WHAT DOES
Mrs. Freeman WANT?

PETROS ABATZOGLOU
Translation by Kay Cicellis

DALKEY ARCHIVE PRESS
NORMAL · LONDON

First published in English by Kedros Publishers,
S.A. Athens, Greece, 1991
Copyright © 1988 by Petros Abatzoglou
English translation copyright © 1991 by Kay Cicellis

First U.S. edition, 2005

Library of Congress Cataloging-in-Publication Data:

Ampatzoglou, Petros, 1931–2004.
  [Ti thelei he kyria Phriman. English]
  What does Mrs. Freeman want? / Petros Abatzoglou ; translation
by Kay Cicellis.
    p. cm.
  ISBN: 1-56478-390-1 (alk. paper)
  I. Tsitsele, Kaie, 1926– II. Title.

PA5612.M6T513 2005
889'.334—dc22

2004063479

Partially funded by grants from the National Endowment for the
Arts, a federal agency, and the Illinois Arts Council, a state agency.

Dalkey Archive Press is a nonprofit organization located at
Milner Library (Illinois State University) and distributed in the
UK by Turnaround Publisher Services Ltd. (London).

www.centerforbookculture.org

Printed on permanent/durable acid-free paper and bound in the
United States of America.

What Does
Mrs. Freeman Want?

ᴀND I REALLY DON'T SEE why we should leave Andros and go off to some other island. What's the point? We've got everything we need here . . . a bedroom with a balcony, clean sheets, a kitchen with a gas oven, two refrigerators, chilled fruit whenever we want it. Everything's just fine. And the view, there's the beautiful little harbor of Batsi right in front of us, with no ferryboats—those dreadful ferryboats that look like horse troughs. Our own little blue harbor, almost boringly blue. It hasn't changed much since last time; there were fewer houses, though, and only one hotel, I seem to remember, with a few windows and a small terrace. I remember that it was Easter and we were staying over there, on the right, next to the baker's shop. Things were rather different in those days, I think. I say "in those days" when I should really be saying "twenty-five years ago."

The awful thing is that the things I remember are all frozen in time. Even the memory of the two of *us,* standing motionless under the tamarisks. So many years ago. Oh, well. It was just after the Easter midnight service, the Resurrection, and we ate *may-iritsa* soup in that little restaurant, our Easter candles still burning . . . The soup was good, real homemade soup, as they say. Not that I'm all that interested in food; I don't need much, as long as it's wholesome and tasty, that's the important thing.

As I was saying, we're doing just fine here, practically alone on our lovely beach; those noisy kids over there will be leaving soon, leave them alone, they're bound to go any minute now. We've got feta cheese—always buy the soft kind—the hard kind won't do, it crumbles like chalk—we've got tomatoes, salt, cucumbers, fresh bread. What else do we need? Besides, remember, flavor chiefly depends on how hungry you happen to be.

So what's the point of going to another island? Go on, tell me. I've found this perfect little spot where I can lie on a bed of seaweed in the shade, while you roast yourself in the sun to your heart's content. This grotto gives off a peculiar damp coolness, and a smell of iodine. I know, it's not really a grotto, but a sort of hollow in the rock, if you like. I just love gazing out of it at the blazing landscape before me; I love drinking my ouzo here. Ouzo is a painkiller, that's what Mrs. Freeman once told me. "Alcohol kills pain," she said. I never used to drink in those days. Mrs. Freeman must be over ninety now. Extraordinary woman; tremendous willpower. If things don't turn out the way she wants them to, she takes it as a personal insult, as downright injustice. But why did I mention Mrs. Freeman? Ah yes. Now I remember—she told me alcohol helps relieve stress, but "Watch it," she said, "it's not a cure." And she was right, too.

Suppose you're feeling anxious, or restless. I mean, you're not getting along with yourself or other people; in short, you're not feeling right. These things happen, there's no explaining them, either you understand what I mean or you don't. So what you do is pour yourself a glass of brandy and gulp it down. Of course, by the time you've reached the point of needing a full glass, you've already become an alcoholic. Goes without saying. You gulp down your brandy and you feel as if you've been struck by lightning. A searing sensation in your throat and all the way down to your stomach. A shudder runs through your body, almost a spasm. Then all at once your body loosens up, and the feeling of relaxation turns into a state of blissful detachment. Everything around you becomes amazingly clear, translucent. It's all very intense, but the main thing is this translucence, this sense of expansion. You feel wonderfully lucid, but cheerful as well. You acquire, as it were, a feeling of benign superiority. All things seem friendly, in a lazy sort of way. A condition halfway between indifference and deep tenderness for everybody and everything. You even look upon yourself with the same friendly feelings, from a distance, as if you were a stranger, as if you stood safely apart and you were out there alone and exposed.

But it only takes the slightest jolt to disrupt this blissful state. Suddenly you remember that one day, three years ago, you came across an old friend of yours who had managed—before dying at the age of fifty-five—to go through a complete range of transformations, starting as a Communist and ending up as a confirmed Greek Orthodox with a fine position in the archbishop's office. In this latest role he went around in a dark suit, bowing and kissing priests' hands; even his voice changed, it turned all mellow and honeyed, you know, full of phony tenderness, as if he were addressing people in distress or on their deathbeds. And to think he was nothing but a shit, I tell you, a perfect shit, you don't often come across such shits; he was clever, of course, but with no particular gift for big plans on a grand scale; he was devoid of imagination, all he wanted was to make do, find himself a snug little place in the sun. So, as I was saying, I happened to meet him and I said hello halfheartedly, and he began gushing at me, "My dear Petros, we've lost touch." "What do you mean by *my dear Petros,*" I said, "you sound like a priest or something." "You mock me because I'm a Christian, but never mind," he said, "one day you'll find the true way, and then your life will be full of loving kindness for your fellow man, because love is all that matters." I just smiled and said, "That may well be, but I'll say goodbye for now." "Goodbye," he said, "and remember, vanity and greed don't lead anywhere, they're a dead end." I smiled once more and walked off.

Well then, as I was saying, after you've gulped down that glass of brandy and you're just beginning to feel relaxed and tolerant and self-sufficient, the blood suddenly rushes to your head, and you fly into a rage because you happen to remember this friend you met in the street. "What do you mean, you bastard," you mutter to yourself, "what do you mean, you filthy bastard, as if I didn't know how you started off, without a penny to your name, never bothering to do an ounce of work, and look at you now, after scheming and pimping and ass-kissing your way up, you've ended up with six shops and four apartments, never mind all those acres of land in popular tourist spots, you scum . . ." But sad to say, you never got round to telling him all this to his face, and now you're in a fit of rage at not having done it. A glass of brandy, even if it doesn't make you drunk, is enough to send you reeling with memories both pleasant and unpleasant. You feel sorry about things you did and about things you didn't do, but not in a detached sort of way—it's as if they were all happening now, in the present. A crazy situation, hard to describe. Well, I might as well have a nip of ouzo. Now Mrs. Freeman, on the contrary, never had any regrets about anything. She always wanted what was good for her as well as for others. Which means she was always right. Later on, after she married Freeman, and after she had given the matter considerable thought, she decided Freeman was also nearly always in the right. Yes, she was extremely fond of him, she respected him as a scholar and admired his integrity, but compared to herself, she considered him simply as a highly intelligent moron. Mrs. Freeman, by the way, never dreams. She plans her life carefully, but she never dreams. Well, let me stop this for the moment.

The tavernas in Batsi are not at all bad. That fish we had yesterday was so fresh. And the stuffed tomatoes were good too. So, as I was saying, after an hour the effect of alcohol begins to wear off, and then you go through an uncomfortable stage—you turn hostile and strangely impatient. As if expecting to go off somewhere, but not knowing or even caring where. At this point, you don't do anything about it, you just wait impatiently. And then comes sadness, as if you had suffered some unendurable loss. And to be precise, there's boredom too, and drowsiness. But if you don't feel like going to sleep just then, all you can do is fill up your glass again. Soon a new burst of euphoria sweeps over you and over your unfortunate friends as well, because drunks usually say clever and amusing things only to other drunks, not just to themselves. Mrs. Freeman never drank. She told me she had tried it once and it made her weep without knowing why.

It bothered her greatly to find herself weeping without reason. She believes one should only cry for a very good reason. She dislikes anything that can't be explained. She said it makes you feel you're at the mercy of some unknown power, a power that governs you and holds you in utter contempt. She always wanted to know what's what, she wanted to be in control. "I'm not interested in daydreams," she said. "I want proof, I want facts." I asked her once if she knew of a specialist who might explain why we fall in love with a particular person, quite often with a person who is far from being *our type.* "No," she answered with a slightly mocking smile, "I don't know of any such specialist, quite simply because no such specialists exist. Some day we'll discover the factors that determine our choice; until then I would advise you to consult a fortune-teller or a medium."

Well, she may be right. In a way I've often envied her cold rationality, her self-confidence. She went through several serious mishaps, illnesses and so on, quite undaunted. She had a number of operations but she simply considered them a temporary nuisance, troublesome minor incidents. "I am, as it were, eternal," she told me quite seriously. "Naturally, only for as long as I'm alive; other people will experience my death, the fact that I am dead—I won't." But what is Mrs. Freeman after? What is it she wants exactly, and what is it she's fighting for so fiercely? I know what you're going to say—that is, if I allow you to put a word in edgewise—we all do the same thing, more or less, fighting on regardless, except that we keep complaining about it, whereas she simply charges ahead, she plays the game cheerfully. But that's not exactly the way things are, and I mean to go into this with you in a moment, but not before I've had another sip of ouzo. It's so pleasant here in the shade, and do you know what, I suggest you take a quick dip in the sea, you're practically baked dry, as good as a crab on the grill, like the ones we used to have at those little tavernas in Chalkis, twenty years ago, I think it was, when we took those people from Zakynthos out to dinner. We piled into the tiny Volkswagen, I remember, all seven of us, and you sat on my lap throughout the long drive, but I didn't feel your weight at all, and as we drove along the coast, we saw restaurants festooned with colored lights; it was as if ships had come ashore with all their lights on.

The charcoal grills were burning away red hot in front of the tavernas, you'd have thought you were in an old-fashioned blacksmith's shop, like the one in Ayia, down by the square. It was Christmas when we first went to Ayia, remember? and there was a fog. Yes, it was Christmas Eve, and the lights in the café had a dim, yellowish glow, and we drank *tsipouro* with olives and pickled peppers. That was years and years ago; in those days, every Saturday the village square filled with donkeys and mules carrying big baskets of vegetables. And there were several blacksmiths, I seem to remember, where horses were taken to be shod, and there was a strong smell of charcoal, but in Chalkis the dominant smell was crab and octopus. There are no more blacksmiths in Ayia now; they've even put a fountain in the square, and there are two cafeterias and one restaurant that serves greasy food. As I was saying, we finally got to Chalkis and ate octopus; only a minute before we had seen its tentacles writhing on the hot grill as if still alive. No, don't get me wrong, I'm not hungry, it's just that I happened to remember the smell. Run along, then, and after you've had a quick swim, I'll explain what I meant when I said that's not exactly the way things are and at this point I've got to admit that I've lost track of what I was going to say, so I'd better have a little ouzo to recover my wits.

WELL, I SHOULD THINK you can see for yourself how much better you feel now that you've come out of the sea, slightly shivering, it must feel so pleasant, like getting over an ordeal, now you can lie down and get warm in the sun; a sort of convalescence, with no obligations, just pure enjoyment.

I like this shivery sensation. But I like the shade even better. Of course, I see your point, it must be wonderful to feel the sun scorching you, burning you through and through, sucking all the moisture out of you. Yes, of course I understand, my dear, but why do you have to subject yourself to what practically amounts to combustion, why grow all dehydrated when there's this lovely shade here, that's what I'd like to know. Ask any desert Arab, or even any ordinary or not so ordinary Arab, and see what he tells you. No, I won't take any part in this form of martyrdom, even though I understand how you feel. I prefer to move into the shade as soon as I'm dry, and then, still cool from the sea, I can get down to the serious business of devouring our fresh bread, our soft feta cheese and tomatoes sprinkled with salt. But I'm digressing from my argument—if I ever had one—I believe I was telling you about Mrs. Freeman. Now Mrs. Freeman takes care to ignore anything that's unpleasant. But then, you're bound to say, who doesn't wish to avoid unpleasantness? Ah, but you see, Mrs. Freeman even refuses to acknowledge its existence. Imagination, she used to tell me, is like a cancerous growth in men's minds, it only leads to disaster. "What's the point of knowing something I am unable to avoid? So I avoid knowing it," she said.

By the way, I remember visiting the London Zoo one day, at feeding time. I walked along the alleys, I saw bored caged animals on either side, I saw birds of prey tearing away at filthy offal, at chunks of blackened meat covered with huge fat flies, leftovers that the proud carnivores (why must we always call them *proud*?) refuse to touch. Then I stopped at the cafeteria for a lukewarm beer and a ham-and-cheese sandwich that tasted like cardboard—watching others eat makes you hungry, you know—and after that I strolled over to a glass cage about two meters high, four square meters all in all, strewn with sand and dry twigs. It was meant to be a sort of miniature desert, I suppose. In a corner, near those twigs and rather like a twig itself, lying in the sand, was a thin, dark-colored snake. It just lay there, inanimate, except for its eyes, which glowed fiercely.

A zookeeper came along, and lifting a sort of wire-netted trapdoor threw a live mouse into the cage. Now you mustn't think this was a cruel, sadistic thing for the keeper to do, no, my dear; unfortunately it so happens this snake produces venom and it needs live flesh to spend it on. The poor innocent little mouse stood there for a moment, stunned; then it rose on its hind legs and began to rub its little pink face with its front feet. It sniffed the air with apparent pleasure and carefully scrabbled around on the sandy floor; obviously, it was soon convinced that this was a safe place because it proceeded to explore the cage, heading first for the glass front, which naturally proved to be impenetrable, and then it made for the dry twigs. The mouse sniffed them cautiously; it picked up the smell of the snake because it suddenly seemed in a great hurry to get away. It trotted back to the spot where the zookeeper had placed it to begin with and concentrated once more on the glass front. At this point the snake, probably prompted by hunger—which for some odd reason appeared to me like sexual hunger, aiming ultimately at ingestion—sprang to life so fast that it became practically invisible. So here was the mouse, wandering like a tourist in an unknown sandy continent, while we spectators looked on from a safe distance, like almighty gods, yes, and stop telling me I always exaggerate whenever I try to describe something, because I'm perfectly aware I do sometimes tend to exaggerate. So here was the mouse, only a few seconds from death, happily sniffing away; I only just had time to say "Don't!" and like a flash, my dear, with lightning speed the invisible snake sank its fangs in the mouse's flank, so that for a moment it looked as if the mouse had acquired a second, enormous tail. The snake retracted and then unfolded itself to an upright position; an upright stick. A brief spasm went through the mouse's body—a quick way out, what we call euthanasia, I suppose. The mouse's eyes dimmed, like steamed-up glass, then the snake swallowed it.

As the mouse slithered down the snake's body, you'd have thought the snake had merely swallowed a small ball. All of a sudden the mouse's death was no longer as momentous as it had appeared a minute ago; the mouse's disappearance even called into question the actual fact of its death. Come to think of it, I believe that our awe and fear of death is partly due to the fact that it happens all at once, it bursts in upon us, upsetting the normal flow of our life with an inexplicable disappearing act. You see, nobody dies by degrees; nobody dies a bit every day. Let's say, a few minutes a day at first, after which you recover and get on with your daily routine; then after a while, you die for an hour a day, then for two hours, for three hours a day, until in about a year you reach the stage of being dead twenty-three hours a day; and finally there comes a moment when your friends and relatives find you looking dead again, only this time they realize what's happened and they remark, "Well, it seems Petros has died for good now; he hasn't come to for two whole days." But we were talking about Mrs. Freeman, who is definitely not a mouse, yet she behaves as if she didn't know one of those twigs is her own personal snake. As a young girl, she told me one day, she saw her grandmother lying in a coffin, between tall flickering candles. Somebody shouted at her—she didn't remember who, she was barely four years old at the time—"Off to bed with you, quick." When she questioned the grown-ups, they told her that Granny had gone away. "She's gone far away," they said, "but she'll come back and bring us chocolate and ice cream and pretty dolls." Ever since then Mrs. Freeman has been convinced that the dead simply go off on a journey; and this journey is a sort of obligation you have to accept, like it or not, but somehow, in some unspecified way, you are guaranteed a return journey. The strange thing is that she actually told me—with a certain air of surprise,

I must admit—that this unquestioning optimism of hers was possibly due to the fact that she had never really loved—or at least depended on—anybody. Not even the violent death of her son made her change her outlook. She always remembered the fatal day he left home in his officer's uniform; he waved to her from a distance and finally disappeared in the faint but persistent drizzle that seeped down like a mist. She never saw him again, and in her mind her son is still traveling somewhere far away, and she could even face the possibility that it was a journey with no return. It was only later, much later, when Freeman died, that she realized this was no ordinary absence, but something irrevocable; she would never see him again, he no longer existed anywhere. She grew scared then. The strange thing is—or perhaps it's not all that strange—she had never been in love with Freeman; all things said, she had never loved him for himself, as a real person named Freeman, but simply as a soft spot she had, or better, an extension of herself. Perhaps what scared her was a sense of her own absence. Yet even then she refused to give in. She kept searching for him in his photographs, she scrutinized them for hours on end. She studied every detail, she identified all the friends and acquaintances who appeared in the photographs with him. In this way she relived with intense pleasure all the years they had spent together. A whole lifetime, reduced to holiday photographs, isolated, disconnected occasions. Never sad occasions, though, because who could possibly want to record such moments in a photograph? She'd smile as she contemplated him in his youth, and later on in his middle age, and at times she'd remonstrate tenderly: "Look at your paunch," she'd say, "you were always much too fond of spaghetti and sweets. If you don't watch out, I'll have a roly-poly husband on my hands." She became something of a recluse and only went out now and then to meet an old friend or acquaintance; but on those rare occasions she always contrived to bring the subject of Freeman into the conversation, no matter what they had been talking about until then: "As Freeman used to say when we were visiting so-and-so . . ." or "By the way, have I ever told you what Freeman did on that rainy afternoon we arrived in Venice? . . ." She went on like this as if Freeman were just around the corner and liable to put in an appearance any moment; exactly as if he were still alive. "Freeman may not agree with me," she'd say, "but that rose tree has got to be removed from the hedge. You know how pig-headed he is. He may seem easygoing, but he isn't. Yes, I know, he never raises his voice or insists on his own point of view, but he gets into a mood, and he keeps it up so stubbornly that in the end you just have to let him have his way."

The last time I saw her she was all wrapped up in reminiscences of their courtship; she recounted with obvious enjoyment how they had fallen in love, how they got married. I may say that by now I know the story of their romance literally by heart. So much so that I often corrected her if she left out a detail during one of her innumerable reminiscing sessions. She would break off then, give me a disarming smile and sigh, "I know, I keep repeating the same things over and over again, but that's the trouble with old people, they all do it—or else choose silence once and for all."

Well then, she was twenty years old when it all began. She was studying linguistics or something of the kind. Freeman happened to hold the chair of linguistics at the time; he was already an eminent figure in his field. You see, scientists and scholars may become famous among their own kind without the world at large ever hearing about them. She was one of his students. A sturdy athletic girl, with intense, pitch-black eyes, madly in love with life. I think I'll just have another ouzo, but please don't interrupt, at this rate we'll never get to the end of Mrs. Freeman's story.

Freeman was thirty-two years old when they met. He had a slim but rather flabby body; his face was unwrinkled, because he never laughed or made faces. He was an undemonstrative sort of person most of

the time, with an innate dislike of highly charged
situations. He liked peaceful surroundings, a room
with all sound shut out, except of course for music,
and even that he kept very low. He loved silence,
the private enjoyment of reading a book, immers-
ing himself in a world of adventures; but in silence,
always. Huge primeval upheavals take place in a
book, great conflicts, inner and outer ones, worlds
are born while you're sitting comfortably in the
peace and quiet of your room, groping blindly for
an occasional sip from the cup of coffee at your side.
He enjoyed good conversation, laced with subtle
undertones and conducted without acerbity; the
kind in which the interlocutors feel their way round
a subject without ever growing too familiar with each
other; disagreeing, yes, but in the sense of a civilized
exchange of views, without the least aggressive intent.
He mistrusted words; words are lethal weapons, he
used to say, they must be handled with care. They
are like mines buried in a lush green meadow, in
which you saunter along in a carefree mood, hum-
ming under your breath, until they suddenly blow
you up sky high. "Words work at you in an under-
handed way," he said. "They insinuate themselves
into your body with cunning tentacles, circulate in
your bloodstream and finally take complete control
of you. You end up as a mere bag of words; words

that act as your stand-in, that shape your character and finally die with you." That was why he was so meticulous in his use of language, like a surgeon fearful of his own scalpel. He often smiled while he talked, as if to encourage his interlocutor, as if to let him know he shouldn't take too seriously what was, after all, no more than a friendly, undemanding exchange. But there were times when this urbane smile of his was misunderstood; people thought he was being sarcastic. His politeness and gentleness were often misconstrued as faintheartedness, but the truth is that he was no coward, though he did tend to evade responsibilities. When he lectured at the University, the way he smiled gave his students the impression that he didn't take them very seriously, or that with a more select audience he would have had more to say; as a result, he sounded somehow as if he were engaged in a soliloquy. Not that he was condescending; on the contrary, students felt free to come up to him, not only to discuss the lecture, but even to consult with him on purely personal matters. He listened attentively and offered his advice after thoughtful consideration. At such moments there was no trace of his customary smile. However, even then he managed to give people the wrong impression perhaps, appearing to speak like an automaton, cold and uninvolved. You see, he wasn't interested in comforting other people, but simply in helping them to understand the situation they were in. Now Mrs. Freeman took good note of all this. She felt greatly tempted to test her youthful good looks and her brains against a man of Freeman's caliber; for Freeman was no unsophisticated youth, undecided and unsettled in his habits; he was the very opposite: a man who had already organized his defenses and chosen the sort of existence that suited him best—on one hand, a dull orderly life in which each day, not to say each hour, was strictly programmed, and on the other, the highly adventurous life that he found in his books. Yet what appeared to be his very self-sufficiency proved an advantage; it helped her to approach him at a more personal level and to insulate him still further from his unresponsive students. Freeman always addressed, or rather taught, his students as a whole, without singling out any one of them; and even this impersonal group he took care to keep at a distance. Now Mrs. Freeman was resolved to make him single her out. She wanted to be loved by a solitary man, in other words by a man who had deliberately singled himself out from the group. Now this happened to be the time when Freeman had just put an end to a comfortable four-year affair with a married woman. There was nothing dramatic about the break-up; it was simply the result of mutual indifference. Without actually realizing it, they stopped seeing each other: one day they didn't bother to mention when they would meet again, they made vague promises to telephone each other, and then came various excuses: urgent work, a bout of flu, an aunt's visit, and so on. To tell the truth, Freeman was slightly annoyed to see how easily Daisy had given him up, but then he found ample compensation in the pleasurable fact that the break-up had been so painless. It was in this unprepared condition that he found himself confronted with Mrs. Freeman.

I LOVE THIS SPOT, seaweed and all. Seaweed has an unusual smell, a pungent smell, I might say. It makes me hungry. Things that smell nice should be edible. Flowers, for instance, have a useless sort of beauty, and I really don't see why they are always thought to represent everything that's delicate and sensitive. I read somewhere, or perhaps I made it up, I'm not sure, that you can make wonderful soup out of seaweed. You boil some rockfish or grey mullet with carrots and celery; when the fish is nearly done, you remove the carrots and celery and throw in the seaweed, just long enough to scald it. You serve the soup with lemon and olive oil, and the whole place will be redolent of the sea. Of course, you've got to wash down the seaweed with ouzo, which reminds me, I'll have another drop for good cheer. The smell of the sea is so delicious—that's why I'm so fond of sea urchins. I've often wondered how sea urchins manage to get all those little pebbles on their backs. But I think I can tell you how—they pick them up one by one with their prickly tentacles. Male sea urchins are black and uninteresting, but the females are lovely, sparkling, multicolored creatures. I love them, alive, or in my stomach. Well, I'd better get back to Mrs. Freeman, ah but I see you're about to go into the sea again.

So, AS I WAS SAYING, Mrs. Freeman now had recourse to an offensive combining both physical and intellectual tactics. First of all, her extraordinary eyes transfixed Freeman without respite, like a relentless battery of laser beams. The first time he was subjected to this frontal attack, he felt nonplussed, and pretended to glance at his notes; he felt as if some great magnetic force had insulated him, encircled him. "This is crazy," he thought, "she can't be looking at me like that, I must have imagined it." So he avoided looking in her direction and gradually calmed down; yet he couldn't help being curious, his attention kept circling round her like a bee, his own voice sounding to him a bit like the buzz of a bee. Finally, as the lecture came to an end, he allowed himself to make contact with her eyes, which immediately released a lethal dose of radiation at him. This time he jerked up as if electrocuted, barely managing to hold on to his desk; he hastily decided that he had better ignore her.

This little game went on for about two weeks. Freeman was fully aware that her eyes were fixed on him, but he stubbornly went on avoiding them. The effort affected his nerves; at home he drank far more coffee than usual; he would interrupt his reading—which had now become a tiresome chore—and stare at the wall, asking himself: "But what is she after? This can't be happening, my breakup with Daisy is probably making me imagine things." At this point, Mrs. Freeman adopted a new line of attack. She switched from trench warfare, as we military people would say, to General Guderian's blitzkrieg, with armored vehicles and 18 and 22 mm guns reducing the chair of linguistics to cinders. Let me explain: the new tactics consisted of questions. What do you mean by this and what do you mean by that—little by little the entire lecture hall seemed to empty, leaving the two of them locked in their erotic combat, oblivious of the common herd.

Mrs. Freeman remained determined; she suspended her passionate scrutiny, but stuck to her guns all the same, this time, however, without her come-hither look or her meaningful hints. And so one late afternoon following an endless discussion, Freeman stood there, still addressing a lecture hall from which his students had discretely departed, while Mrs. Freeman faced him from the floor, upright, tenderly attentive, like a mother listening to her infant reciting a cute little poem—"Jack and Jill went up the hill . . ."—when he suddenly came to his senses, smiled his old familiar smile and suggested they have coffee together in the tearoom across the street.

It was a dingy, run-down place, dirty beyond belief, not visibly so, but more as if the dirt steamed up from the very chinks and cracks in the place. Everything was smeared with grime, like a coating of fat that has been used for frying fish and chips. The pale lights, too, were unspeakably depressing.

They sat at a corner table. A little old man in a clean, frayed suit sat at the next table, solemnly devouring a slice of apple pie and drinking tea. "Funny, wasn't it," Mrs. Freeman said to me, "that my first date with the famous professor should have taken place in a tearoom meant for customers in a hurry, not bothered by the seediness of the place, only wanting a quick snack, and then running off."

This time Mrs. Freeman made the first move. She volunteered a series of remarks on Freeman's lecture; she explained that, in her view, words leave room for a degree of interpretation; they are certainly not autonomous—they are simply the answer to some need, a human need, it goes without saying. It is human need that produced words in the first place; now, whether one person says *Mother* and another *Mutter* or *Madre* doesn't make any difference. In brief, words are the projection of our own needs. Astounded, yet fascinated, Freeman listened to his young student as she gave him a very succinct summary of his entire course; the strange thing was that he found this perfectly natural and wasn't for a moment tempted to laugh at her presumption. He just sat there, drinking his watery coffee, and stared at her spellbound. But after a while Mrs. Freeman realized she was overdoing it; it also occurred to her that the tearoom was not exactly the right place for further developments, or, to put it plainly, for more intimate effusions. Behind the counter, the waiter seemed to take a keen interest in them, not even bothering to conceal it. So she decided to put an end to the meeting before things got awkward. She mumbled an excuse and disappeared.

Now I must admit I've no idea what made me start this story about Mrs. Freeman. I always feel very surprised when I start telling a story because I usually do it without any particular motive in mind; I suppose what triggers me is something quite insignificant that happens to bring back a long-forgotten incident. The funny thing is that I haven't the slightest interest in Mrs. Freeman at the moment; I'm not in the least concerned with what she did or didn't do. And I'm puzzled, deeply puzzled, because I keep referring to her as *Mrs.* Freeman, after I've known her for so long. I'm sure it's not out of respect, because if a close friend called me *Mr.* Abatzoglou, and especially if he emphasized the Mister, I would waste no time answering back, "Don't you Mister me, you slob. If that's your idea of making fun of me . . ." That's what I would say, I know the likes of them, handing out "dear sirs" right and left, manipulating honest people; faceless, mummified types drenched in eau-de-cologne to cover up the stench of their oh-so-clean skins; you know the types I mean, mouthing "ladies-and-gentlemen" with such obvious enjoyment, I'll put them up against the wall some day and have them shot, but then I'll have to shoot the executioners, and then who will be left to execute me?

Stupid of me to lose my temper like that. As I was telling you, it's the way alcohol affects your brain. Storms start raging through your cerebral cells and all your nerve endings go berserk at the screwy messages they're receiving. I might even say the effect is like an enormous explosion, something like those magnetic solar storms we hear about; all this puts a tremendous strain on your system, the poor thing hasn't a clue what all this insane activity is about. The alcoholic's face turns into a leper's mask, something like *leontiasis*; the muscles slacken, all expression is frozen, the eyes go glassy. But in contrast to the expressionless face, the body becomes possessed by an unwonted agitation, an uncoordinated mobility, like a dog who has lost the scent and no longer knows which way to go.

So—according to what Mrs. Freeman told me— the next day her husband-to-be began his lecture with his usual impassive air. He carried on his monologue with what looked like studied indifference, but as the minutes went by, he began to betray signs of anxiety; something had gone wrong, he seemed irritated by his own composure. Then all of a sudden, upon being required to interpret the verbs *to feel* and *to desire,* he burst into a purely erotic discourse, always under Mrs. Freeman's searing stare, which followed him relentlessly like a spotlight through his free-for-all gala performance. In short, he delivered a whole pack of worn-out platitudes. He told his bemused, not to say petrified, students that unless words express emotion, indeed passion, they are nothing more than dead matter. A person who uses words without investing them with feeling is simply a machine producing a string of consonants and vowels. By this time he was practically shouting, possessed by a rage that was entirely gratuitous, since no one had dared raise any objections to what he was saying. He banged his fist on the desk. "He who loves not," he said, "is a crippled being, for words exist only as a means of partaking in love. Living words are love." Mrs. Freeman listened attentively, inwardly rejoicing. "Yes, my sweet, yes, my baby, yes, yes, my love, go on talking, I love you and you love me, so talk away . . ."

Well, the lecture eventually came to an end, and Freeman was left standing there, all passion spent. He realized he had behaved rashly; he had used his position as a lecturer as an excuse to make a scholarly, yet blatant, declaration of love, not unlike a foolish adolescent. He was upset, full of shame, for he sensed that Mrs. Freeman knew perfectly well that he had been talking about his feelings for her and not about anything as universal as psycholinguistic mechanisms. All right, my dear, I won't try to define what I mean by psycholinguistic mechanisms but don't interrupt, because I'll lose track of my thoughts—there, I *have* lost track, what was I saying? Ah, yes, Freeman's shame. So he literally fled, head down, firmly resolved to remain cool and aloof—at least for the next day or two—if he should happen to meet her. He also decided to do his best to avoid such a meeting. But you see, my dear, Mrs. Freeman was no ordinary woman; she wasn't one of those silly suburban girls who enjoy reading cheap magazines like *Donna*—now how the hell do you expect me to know that's a brand of sanitary napkins?—the kind of magazines with photo layouts and stories about rich men falling in love with penniless girls. Mrs. Freeman is a woman with a very powerful personality; she realized at once that it was her turn to humble herself a bit in order to counterbalance the humiliation he had just suffered. A superior hand, if it is over-conspicuous, she told me once, discourages its adversary and may even drive him to abandon the game.

Freeman was by no means a cold fish, sexually speaking; as a matter of fact, his fantasies were pornographically inclined, as I found out—but he was severely afflicted with timidity. Being a scholar, anything that had to do with straightforward action filled him with dread. Despite his orgiastic imagination, he panicked at the thought of taking the initiative. He suddenly discovered all kinds of physical defects in his person: his body was ugly; his arms were too long; his nose was—I don't know what his nose was; in short, he grew paralyzed with fear. As a temporary lover, he would have proved an all-time fiasco. Gripped with panic, he rushed into hiding, longed to bury himself, to disappear into the remotest recesses of his house. But Mrs. Freeman, like a tigress stalking her victim, whiskers quivering in exquisite anticipation, lay in ambush behind some shrubs in the University grounds. Suddenly she pounced and stood in Freeman's way. Her sharp young claws pinned him to the spot, her little pink tongue darted gleefully across her lips . . .

The sun's almost unbearably hot today, unusually so, I'd say. It's because there's no breeze. Look at the sea stretching out there, pale, almost milky, where it meets the sky. I wouldn't be surprised if it all evaporated, leaving us stranded here to watch the fish floundering in the dry seaweed or on the muddy seabed. It reminds me of the sea in Tunisia; the heat was incredible, 40° Centigrade; and I felt a tightening in my chest as I watched the crowd piling into that ancient creaking boat which seemed about to fall to pieces at any moment. We were relegated to the upper deck, I remember. I began to feel desperate; what a frightful situation it was; we were herded in that boat like goats. It even crossed my mind that once we reached Marseilles—*if* we ever reached it, that is—they would fling us onto the pier as I once saw them do in Volos with a boatload of wild goats, the kind that graze on barren islands, surviving on dry thistle but no water, perhaps licking a few drops of dew off the ground, or even sea water. This is what makes their flesh so good to eat, they say. Poor creatures, in winter they're at the mercy of raging gales, no shelter anywhere on those desert islands, deserts indeed; in summer the sun beats down on them mercilessly, the ground sends off heat like burning metal, it's unbearable. The wild goats in Volos—smaller than the domestic ones—were carelessly flung onto the concrete waterfront. Some of them had their legs broken in the process and bleated agonizingly. So, I thought, what if they unload us along with the Tunisians onto the pier like goats? They had kept us confined on deck without water, the toilet was disgusting, filthy water sloshing in and out like the tide. Most of the passengers were Tunisian workers, you see; in the eyes of the French they're no better than animals. And yet, do you remember what fun we had that night on board, with singing and music, and how we went to sleep half-drunk, like soldiers in some godforsaken outpost, stacked in a row close to each other, the wind sneaking in through the seams of our sleeping bags? Next morning, out of the blue, we caught sight of Marseilles. The sea was like warm soup, and soup was what we had for supper on the waterfront in Marseilles, bouillabaisse, but I found it disappointing. It had tasteless little fish floating around in it, bristling with nasty bones, and two miserable little crayfish that looked as if they were made of plastic. The broth itself was pure dishwater. Couldn't compare to Anna's fish soup; no wonder, she uses two kilos of fish for four people, fresh tomatoes, whole onions, celery. Perfectly delicious, eaten piping hot under the trees on a moonlit night, or even a moonless one. You're damn right, I am hungry, my dear, I'm only human, even if it doesn't show much.

Well then—Mrs. Freeman smiled at the professor, but she stood her ground with a very determined look, forcing him to face her. "If you have a few minutes to spare," she said, with a masterly show of false diffidence, "what would you say to a drink at Vicker's? I went there once and rather liked it, but it's no fun going there alone. They serve lovely chicken liver patties, and mashed potatoes with German sausage, and apple pie with heaps of apple in it."

She played the innocent little girl, pretended she knew nothing about the massacre, I mean the lecture. In other words she put on a Little Red Riding Hood act, when she was actually the Wolf and Freeman the unfortunate Granny. Only a minute ago, the famous professor had cringed in terror at the thought that he had irrevocably made a complete fool of himself; so now he jumped at her offer with relief. He said neither yes nor no, but simply followed her. He thought it was a wonderful idea, and once they got there he agreed the apple pie was indeed as good as home-made, obviously fresh from the oven, and the chicken patties, too, were really tasty, exactly like the ones they used to make in the old days in Hampshire or Hertfordshire or some shire or other, he said. It was a pleasant pub; there were dozens of sparkling glasses standing in endless rows on shelves or hanging from hooks above the bar, in front of mirrors in which they proliferated in endless reflections. In these pubs, you know, you get the impression that all those glasses are thirsty, they look like gaping thirsty mouths prompting you to go on drinking and drinking.

They paused in front of the food on display, their interest definitely roused, and examined the various dishes: steaming hot pies, Irish stew, rosy ham garnished with sliced tomatoes, cucumber and lettuce. There weren't any customers yet; the barman seemed to be limbering up for a display of professional efficiency. He rubbed away furiously with a napkin at every object within sight, as if there were indelible stains to be dealt with all over the place. The floor was covered with a wall-to-wall maroon carpet, under which another world teemed, a microcosm ruled by its own laws, heaving with cataclysmic wars, copulation, birth, death; yet alive with a mechanical life, devoid of hatred or love, a purely material process, nothing more.

As I was saying, the Freemans gazed at the food greedily and finally ordered their dinner, after mutual consultation, like a couple who have been living together for years and enjoy treating themselves occasionally to a simple meal at the pub.

But I'd like to tell you about a thought that has just flashed across my nimble mind. As you may have noticed, so far I've always called Mrs. Freeman "Mrs. Freeman," even though she was not yet married to Freeman, yet I have never once referred to him as "Mr. Freeman." Why? I don't really know. For all his fame, I think of him somehow as a parasitical plant clinging to a wall. He was a scholar, in other words a man who observed creative people with keen interest. I might even say he also observed words, the great expeditionary force of words, and described their behavior in detail, always from the point of view of a mere observer. He loved words, but they pointedly ignored him. He didn't dare become familiar with them, let alone make love to them. And so it was that words assumed the air of prim, respectable ladies; they addressed him with genteel decorum, they watched their manner and appearance, they never got cross with him, they never flew into a temper or lashed out at him tooth and nail; in short, they secretly laughed at him. They sat at their desks, as good as gold, and wearily repeated after him whatever he happened to be dictating. There was nothing he could do about it: Freeman was like something aborted by a computer. His relationship with the world at large was that of a man who keeps disinfecting himself out of disgust for what he is as well as for what he is not.

At the time we're speaking about, Freeman was officially registered under his real name, whereas Mrs. Freeman's name was Margaret. I don't believe she had a surname, she was only Margaret, just as one says: the "Queen." Margarets are Margarets, and we all have some touching incident to recount about a Margaret. We remember our Margarets with a touch of sadness, with deep emotion, we can just glimpse them smiling at us, like little girls clutching their dolls, playing hide-and-seek with us. Margarets remain girls forever, unalterable girls, though some day later on they may change into Mrs. Freemans, and that is the end of them. The transmutation is final, there goes our beloved Margaret. But let's get on with the story.

THEY SAT IN SEMI-DARKNESS at a small marble table with a wooden edge. Mrs. Freeman smiled rather shyly, I might even say tenderly. She was in no mood to show off or play tricks. On the contrary.

Of course, she didn't put on the little schoolgirl act; she simply offered the famous professor a chance to take the initiative. So she gazed at him sweetly, but meaningfully as well. You must forgive me if I point out something you probably know already, but never mind, we know a great many things but that doesn't mean we should never talk about them. What I wanted to say is that people can communicate perfectly well with their eyes; they can use their eyes not only to express some particular point, but also abstract thoughts. Our eyes are engaged in endless conversations. I often can't help laughing to myself as I watch young couples sitting together: the boy usually talks non-stop, explaining, persuading, emphasizing, and then explaining all over again, while the girl gazes at him wide-eyed as if probing into his very soul, as if enraptured by all his idiotic pronouncements; whether he is a doctor or an engineer, a policeman or a lawyer, he makes it sound as if he never makes a mistake, he speaks his mind to his superiors, courageously and uncompromisingly, so that in the end they all congratulate him, vastly impressed by his sterling quality. The girl doesn't care one way or another, and she's quite right, too. As a female friend once told me, a man who is not in love usually sits there stolidly, not saying much; but if he's excited, he becomes garrulous, there's no way you can stop him.

He feels he's got to talk you into intimacy, never realizing there's no need, you've already accepted him, and you're perfectly willing to make love or even start a long-term affair.

But in Freeman's case it was different: he had already worn himself out during the lecture; he had been left totally defenseless under the barrage of laser beams emitted by Mrs. Freeman's eyes. So all he could do now was go on and on about "What will you have, a gin and tonic perhaps, what about orange juice or a cocktail or a beer?" while she merely repeated, "Whatever you like, whatever you're having"; until Freeman began to stammer in a panic and finally ordered whiskey for both of them, without consulting her this time. He ordered a double whiskey for himself and gulped it down almost in one swallow, and immediately ordered another one, and then a third one. You'd have thought he was preparing himself for open-heart surgery without an anesthetic. He was not used to hard liquor; he usually stuck to milky tea. When working at home, he took a break every half hour or so, and like a small child gleefully setting out to steal chocolates, he went through the ritual of making himself a mug of tea; sighing in anticipation, he carried it to his study and then, with proper concentration, he took his first sip. But now, under the powerful influence of whiskey, he lost control completely, as if some stranger had taken possession of him. He grew outrageously self-confident, his words tumbled out in an almost incoherent stream, while he remained under the impression that he was making some very important statements. He admitted without difficulty that his lecture had been ridiculous, but added that behind this laughable façade she must have sensed an appealing human quality about him. Then he suddenly began to reel off another lecture about words. This time he seemed to be engaged in a fierce argument with them, as if they were his mortal enemies, as if they had betrayed him and mocked him and sought to expose him by means of continuous shifts of meaning. In short, he insisted that words are independent entities, practically existing on their own, unaffected by us humans, like spirits endowed with magic properties that we happened to discover at some point, but which existed long before we came on the scene.

Mrs. Freeman was at a loss. She had no trouble understanding the powerful, liberating influence of love, but she was totally ignorant of the tremendous power of alcohol. Freeman appeared to her as a warlike, aggressive male brimming with resolve. Astounded, she listened to him asserting that words can only mean what we mean them to mean; which is to say that he refuted what he had said only a minute ago, offering as an example the Greek word *ethnos* (nation), which to the ancient Hellenes meant something like *species*. The "nation of bees," the "nation of cats," and so on. Later on, there emerged the word *ethnikos* (national), which was a term of abuse, meaning *idolater, Gentile*. It was only much later, in its French form, that the word *nation* was made respectable, as it became identified with patriotism. In recent years, of course, it has become a derogatory term once again, at least for a large number of people, since it is now associated with mindless chauvinism. As he ranted on, he gripped her right hand as if wanting to tear it off and take it home with him as a souvenir. At this point, however, he felt drained, exhausted, and turned his face to the window.

The yellow streetlights were on. There was a faint, diffuse fog hanging in the air. It seems funny to mention fog as I sit in my lovely cave gazing out at the shimmering sunlight and the bright water, feeling I could stay here forever and go on talking without end.

Freeman paused, tired and happy, convinced he had done his duty. Mrs. Freeman touched his hand gently. "Let's go now, shall we?" she said. Freeman, his white flag held high, escorted her home. She gave him a feathery kiss on the lips and disappeared, closing the door slowly behind her.

Freeman made his way home like a sleepwalker. He undressed absentmindedly, a stranger to himself, he threw his clothes on the floor: this meticulous man, who could not tolerate any form of disorder, didn't give a damn about such things anymore. He felt an intense urge to do something, but he wasn't sure what. Suddenly he felt—he literally *felt,* that is the word— that he had lost the ability to think, that he could no longer form meaningful sentences. He was adrift in a flow of feelings, swirling currents of unformulated desires, a sort of terror racing through him, a revolu- tion perhaps—the hitherto disciplined army of words rising up in arms. High-ranking officers gesticulated angrily, verbs and adjectives abandoned their horses and went off for a nap, while the infantry—puny conjunctions and prepositions—deserted and took to the mountains, to the sea, the hot summer, the kisses of youth. All this turmoil turned into imagery. Fleeting images at play, free and happy, devoid of continuity or remorse. Freeman made a half-hearted effort to straighten things out, to restore law and order, to make excuses for himself ("I've had a bit too much to drink perhaps") in the hope of gather- ing the dispersed troops that he had spent so many years of selfless dedication trying to organize; but the rebels had won the day; horrified, he heard a voice in his head uttering words totally unacceptable to any self-respecting scholar, let alone a linguist: "Go fuck yourself, you jerk, get rid of your pretentiousness."

"A fine state of affairs," he thought, "now just you try proving there are such things as God, justice, truth, consistency, continuity, causality. Try proving you're a rational creature who knows the meaning of life and—why not?—death." He flung himself on his bed and the only thought that lingered in his mind before falling asleep was: "I must buy her a rose tomorrow . . . She'll understand . . ."

Next morning he found himself in excellent spirits. His intoxicated troops returned meekly to camp, slightly abashed, and even proceeded to align themselves in spectacular formations, by turns poetical or philosophical. Indeed, a number of words were forthwith promoted to higher ranks, words like *love, tenderness, bright eyes,* while whole sentences were demoted, as for instance: "After due consideration, I have reached the conclusion that . . ." or "This view does not necessarily represent a definitive assessment of the question under discussion . . ." He felt like a man in love, ready to take on the whole world, if need be. In her room Mrs. Freeman felt the same; she too was in love and capable of anything.

So there they were, the two of them, caught in waves of love that washed over them and raised their temperature sky high, both possessed by a burning desire to tear the beloved one to pieces, to devour, ingest, put the beloved one in their pocket, heart, mouth, to transplant and appropriate the beloved as a third arm, foot, kidney; both of them, I say, writhing in the throes of passion, yet carefully preparing their weaponry, putting on their iron gauntlets and plumed helmets, planning their tactical moves in anticipation of an imminent encounter in the University quadrangle—that maniacally cropped patch of lawn where no flowers are ever allowed to grow—both of them, I say, anticipating the moment when with thumping heart and a sick feeling in the pit of the stomach they would begin their duel, using light thrusts of the sword without meaning to cause injury or even to win the upper hand, but simply as a friendly gesture, simply as a mutual encouragement to carry their bloodless confrontation through to the end.

In her room Mrs. Freeman scanned her face grimly in the mirror for any vulnerable spot that might give Freeman a chance for victory. She scrutinized her body with the eyes of a fastidious buyer or a professional pimp. And Freeman, who had long since given up the practice of self-perusal, changed his shirt several times; he wanted something youthful, yet respectable enough to avoid eliciting unfavorable (or worse) comments at the University. What he needed was a pleasantly neutral appearance. He also attempted to put together a few well-chosen, tactful phrases conveying a certain degree of intimacy, the sharing of a tacit agreement, a secret; but he did not make much headway in this direction. In the end he opted for a warm, breezy spontaneity. Meanwhile, Mrs. Freeman had problems of her own. Her sensuality was not obvious, she was not the kind of woman who by her mere presence can bring about what is known as an accomplished fact; she needed first to establish an atmosphere of friendliness and trust. On the other hand, Freeman was not your typical male either—sex for the sake of sex, as they say—as a matter of fact, as I gathered from gossip, sex made him feel uncomfortable, he considered it an offensive practice, in a way, like urinating in a public place and not even paying a fine for it. He was a sexual creature, but he was ashamed of his sexuality. "I can't say how much I really loved him," Mrs. Freeman told me when she was nearing ninety. "I don't really remember." She had his photograph hanging above her desk, like an old garment on a hanger that you haven't quite made up your mind to discard, but that you don't really want to wear either. The fact was that she did love him when she told me this, though in an abstract sort of way perhaps; anyway, she talked of nothing else. She spent her whole time reminiscing about Freeman; he was her only companion; I might even say that her only purpose in life was remembering Freeman.

As I was saying then, they both sprinted forth in a headlong race towards their fateful encounter. The weather was friendly, perfect for lovers, ready to lend a helping hand: a clear sky, free of cloudy blemishes; warm spring sunshine; flowering shrubs with bright, fresh colors. The situation presented all the prerequisites to make the encounter a complete success, except for one important drawback: Mrs. Freeman's lack of experience in love. She had had a number of romantic skirmishes of course as a girl, and not long ago she had been involved in a harmless flirtation with a fellow student; but this was the first time she had really fallen in love. To tell the truth, she had been relatively cool-headed when she first set her sights on Freeman; she hadn't even realized how serious her feelings were. It had all seemed like a game at first; but on the morning she stood in front of the mirror examining her body, she suddenly discovered she was in love. All the way to the lecture hall she felt quite normal, no morbid symptoms at all, but when she saw him entering the lecture hall, she felt faint, she began to sweat and her heart raced uncontrollably. The familiar Professor Freeman had changed into St. George on horseback striking at the accursed dragon, as depicted by Cello.

Now that is a painting I am extremely fond of; I would love to have it hanging in my room. Do you know what the only test I use is when judging a painting? I question myself very rigorously: "Tell me, would you hang this picture in your room or wouldn't you?" A painter's fame is of course very useful for commercial reasons, and I'd very much like to own a Rubens, a Rembrandt, a Raphael or an El Greco; I'd sell them right away at Sotheby's or Christie's and pocket my lovely millions of dollars or pounds and become stinking rich without ever missing *The Night Watch* or the coronation of some Louis or other riding away on a mare called Europe. But I can't say the same for Goya. Perhaps I would end up selling him too, but with a certain amount of regret; I'd really like to have him in my room.

So when Mrs. Freeman saw him walk into the lecture hall, she was immediately struck by the thought: "This is love—it's a kind of disease, it seems." She watched him intently as he delivered his lecture with his usual neutral aplomb, a bright halo round his head. Freeman had put his emotions in order by then, so he lectured on placidly without once glancing in her direction, like a man who can confidently put aside something that he now considers his own. As the minutes went by, Mrs. Freeman's panic grew, and as the professor was about to collect his notes and wish his students good day with that well-known smile of his, she rushed out of the lecture hall and ran all the way to her room, a few blocks away from the University.

It was a nice little attic room; the walls were covered with posters, some of them political, others advertising concerts and plays, adding a colorful note. She lay down on her bed, shut her eyes and tried to sort out her troubled thoughts. She admitted she had lost her nerve; Freeman had suddenly seemed inaccessible; how could he possibly take her seriously after the foolish way she had behaved! She was annoyed with herself; then vexation gave way to anxiety; she very nearly burst into tears as she recalled how she had dared lecture Freeman on linguistic matters. She remembered how she had sat opposite him in the tearoom, holding forth about words as if addressing a schoolboy, instead of—The Famous Professor Freeman, of all people! She imagined him laughing condescendingly as he told his friends about the incident: "And then this young thing began making comments on the lecture I had given them that morning, but naturally she made a complete mess of it . . ." I'll never see him again, she cried, drumming her fists on the bed, I'll go away, I've made an utter fool of myself. Locked away in her room, she spent the day reading passages from Freeman's book, literally ill with worry and humiliation. And the more she read, the more ashamed she felt.

But wait and see what happened to Freeman. In a sprightly, elated mood, as becomes a hopeful suitor, he rushed off to the park as soon as the lecture was over. He could still feel on his lips the light kiss Mrs. Freeman had given him the night before; he saw it as a promise, a contractual bond. He looked right, he looked left—no sign of Mrs. Freeman. He walked on; she was nowhere to be seen. He strolled along the street, checked in at the tearoom. No sign of her. He felt disappointed, deflated; his spirits fell, but then he told himself that she had probably had some urgent business to attend to, they hadn't actually made an appointment, no need to jump to conclusions. He whistled a cheerful tune under his breath. He walked back slowly to the tearoom and sipped his coffee in long lingering sips at a table next to the window, where he was framed like a portrait, visible to all passersby; after which he returned to the University on the pretext of having forgotten a book he was sure to need for tomorrow's lecture. On the way back he paused in front of every shop window, staring hard at displays of kitchenware, electrical appliances, garden furniture, clothes, toys, and ended up in a pub. Once again he chose to sit in a conspicuous place where he could see and be seen.

He had a hasty meal of sausages and mashed potatoes and spent forty-five minutes drinking a single mug of beer. He eventually made his way home, ostensibly as cheerful and carefree as ever.

I needn't tell you, of course, that he didn't read a line that day, let alone glance at the newspaper. He wanted to kick himself for not having thought of asking for her telephone number. This unhappy state of affairs continued on the following days. Mrs. Freeman kept away from the University, wavering between despair and wild hope. As despair prevailed in the end, she took up with her fellow student again, just for the sake of having someone to talk to. When they met, she would often fall silent, and then walk off suddenly without a word of explanation. They had made love once at a party, quickly and clumsily, probably both half-drunk and this made her loathe him, sexually speaking, I mean, while it had the opposite effect on the student—he fell in love with her, that's life for you. No, don't interrupt or I'll forget what I was going to say. She was quite fond of him, or rather she was touched by the way he nosed round her sorrowfully like a sick animal. During this critical period, Freeman was also reduced to a state of despair. Diffident, apprehensive, he just couldn't make up his mind what to do. In the end he managed to get hold of her telephone number; he resolved to call her if she didn't turn up at the University the next day. He was about to declare his love at last, on the telephone, if need be. But this also happened to be the day when the student chose to declare his love, and the day when Mrs. Freeman decided she would go to the lecture and bravely confront her professor. So there we have all three of them waiting in the wings to play the crucial scene of the grand finale.

IT SO HAPPENED that the student found some encouragement in the fact that Mrs. Freeman had accepted him as her exclusive companion for the past few days; what was more, she had given him a quick kiss the night before—a farewell kiss as it turned out, though she didn't realize it at the time. So he asked her to meet him around noon at the tearoom opposite the University; there was a very serious matter he wanted to discuss with her, he insisted. Mrs. Freeman had no trouble guessing what the serious matter was, and she felt sad because she had used the boy to practice her amorous skills, to test her powers; she had tried to picture him in the role of lover and companion, better still, as the future father of her children. The whole performance had been but a rehearsal for the actual mating of Mrs. Freeman.

All these past days she had been dreaming up her own little cosmogony, she had been preparing her contribution to the perpetuation of the species, that and nothing more.

WELL, I MIGHT AS WELL HAVE ANOTHER OUZO. Just the thing to make you sleep well. But who do they think they are, the Mrs. Freemans of this world? Do they really think their decisions are so important? What fancy trappings, what elaborate disguises they use, changing at will into mice, elephants, kangaroos, vipers, fish floating around in an aquarium, their exotic colors glittering misleadingly in the water, like shiny pebbles that grow dull when put out to dry and turn out to be ordinary stones.

THE STUDENT, THEN, declared his love in hesitant tones, with long and frequent pauses, after giving Mrs. Freeman a detailed description of his symptoms: no appetite, lack of concentration, daydreams centering on her, always featuring the two of them making plans for the future. But that was not all; there were sudden fits of depression, with clinical symptoms: a thumping heart whenever he saw a girl vaguely like her walking in the distance; and insomnia, punctuated with frequent sighs. Hearing about these symptoms, Mrs. Freeman took it upon herself—with a great deal of patience, it must be admitted—to convince the student, or rather to compel him, almost aggressively, to acknowledge that he wasn't truly in love with her. "Let's not exaggerate," she said; "yes, those are certainly signs pointing to a predisposition of falling in love, but it isn't real love." The young man assumed that she was using these arguments to cover up the fact that she doubted his love, so he returned to the attack even more forcefully, which caused Mrs. Freeman to resort to emergency surgery without anesthesia. In other words, she told him bluntly that she was not in love with him nor ever would be, to the end of time. And what do you think happened at this very moment? A devilish coincidence is what I would call it.

Coincidences can sometimes prove fatal to a relationship, which reminds me of a certain afternoon long ago: I was eighteen, and a girl called Maria, aged fifteen, radiantly beautiful in my youthful eyes, moved into the house next door with her parents. It all started with furtive glances and a few monosyllables; we even managed to form brief sentences like "how are you getting on with ancient Greek verbs?"

Eventually I scraped together a few drachmas and took her to the cinema. I didn't see much of the film, I just enjoyed sitting next to her, I was in a sort of trance. At a certain point, when it looked as if the hero were in serious danger, I squeezed her hand meaningfully. She abandoned it in mine like a tepid, dead fish. Well, we went out together two or three more times, I even got around to kissing her, and that day I walked home exhilarated and gulped down a bowl of baked beans with olives and onion. On the following afternoon, feeling very much like a young man who is about to embark on an "affair," I went for a long walk to the Anafiotika quarter, at the foot of the Acropolis. And as I was strolling along without a care in the world, weaving plans around my newborn love, I caught sight of her with a young man; he was holding her hand, and as if that wasn't bad enough, he stooped and gave her a fleeting kiss. I walked home feeling very sorry for myself. From that day on I deliberately avoided her; if we happened to meet, I greeted her coldly and rushed away as if being chased. One day she stopped me in the street. "I haven't seen you for ages," she said, "you must be awfully busy." I nodded, without looking at her and turned away. The family moved soon afterwards and we lost touch. And then suddenly, twenty years later, I came upon her at a stupid lecture by some French writer of the bantamweight class (as we boxers are in the habit of saying); this man went on and on for what seemed like ages, so I suggested we leave and have coffee somewhere together. She told me about her marriage, her children; then just before we parted—for good this time, I hoped—she turned to me and said: "I'd like to ask you something—I can't help being curious: what happened all those years ago to make you stop courting me and to disappear so suddenly?" I told her about the afternoon I saw her with that young man at the foot of the Acropolis. She burst out laughing. "I never liked that boy much, it was you I wanted; you could at least have asked me." Devilish coincidences, as I said. Like that split second just after Mrs. Freeman had finished slashing the poor student's feelings to bits. Feeling sorry for him, she clasped his hand, while he gazed at her with an adoring look: that was the very moment when . . . guess who walked past the tearoom, just you guess. Yes. Of course. Freeman. At this point I should explain that sixty or seventy years ago, girls didn't normally struggle into their knickers on the beach in the presence of men, or lie down in the sun with their breasts bare, as you are doing now, bless you. Nowadays even kissing somebody on the mouth only means you're in a friendly mood, at the very most; and even that is open to question. But in those days, the spectacle of Mrs. Freeman holding hands with the student struck Freeman as a public declaration of love, no less, almost as bad as watching his beloved lying naked on a table and having sex with someone else in full view of customers drinking coffee with assumed indifference so as not to embarrass the lovers.

Hot waves surged in his head, he literally saw red, like seeing the world through tinted glass; then the waves receded, leaving him with an ice-cold sensation, completely drained of blood. His arms hung paralyzed at his sides; only his legs retained their ability to move, and rushing to the rescue dragged their owner away from the hideous spectacle. Breathless, he took refuge in his room, like a wounded animal, I might say, if I wanted to sound original, in the manner of so many authors who believe they can impress their readers with striking comparisons of this kind. Of course, they do manage to impress *some* readers, but then they are the sort an author can easily do without.

Freeman rummaged in his kitchen cupboard till he discovered a half-full bottle of whiskey tucked away at the back, probably kept there for medicinal purposes; he hardly ever touched the stuff. Now he took long generous drinks of it, like someone committing suicide; he emptied the bottle, sat down on his bed, stared round the room in a daze, and passed out.

As you may have realized, things were taking a nasty turn. Freeman did not go to the University on the following day. He lay groaning in bed, feeling horribly ill. As for Mrs. Freeman, she had an anxious time of it, too. She had already visualized the scene of her return to the lecture hall; she had decided to stop playing hard to get, to put aside her foolish vanity and reveal her true feelings at last. Both of them felt almost unhappy, yes, I said almost, and don't you interrupt me with why *almost,* because *almost* means that nothing irrevocable had happened, yet. The next day Freeman rose from his bed in a cadaverous state and went to the University, looking like something out of Madame Tussaud's. I've never been able to understand why tourists go and spend good money on that unspeakably boring exhibition, all those celebrities have such a dusty look, and being made of wax makes them seem smaller than life-size. I admit I once went to Madame Tussaud's myself, but only because my godson dragged me there; he was only twelve years old, so I've forgiven him.

Freeman began his lecture, his hands shaking, his papers in a mess, his voice unsteady, a bewildered look on his face as if he could hardly believe the words issuing from his own mouth. Pale and confused, he thought he had been resuscitated temporarily for the sole purpose of this lecture, only to go back quietly to his grave the moment it was over. He was so certain Mrs. Freeman wouldn't be present that he didn't even cast a casual glance at the place she usually occupied. Mrs. Freeman, on the other hand, totally ignorant of what had gone on before—his witnessing the hand-holding scene, the half-bottle of whiskey—concluded that he must be feeling hurt and angry with her. She was amazed to see a perfectly rational, healthy man reduced to such a state in the space of a few days. Unable to believe her eyes, she watched him collect his notes clumsily at the end of the lecture, stuff them in his briefcase and stagger away, remote and ashen-faced, oblivious of his surroundings, like a man pursued by a noonday Dracula. There was something distinctly odd about it. The natural thing for him to do would be to come up to her and ask her what had happened to her, why she had been absent all these days. He had the look of someone who has been through an ordeal of some sort. What had she done to him, what had she said last time they met? What had gone wrong? Freeman was not the man to nurse a petty grievance. He looked as if he had surrendered to a fate against which he was utterly defenseless. These thoughts kept cropping up in her mind as she munched her apple pie listlessly in the tearoom. She was with a girlfriend who chattered endlessly about clothes. Mrs. Freeman listened to her as one listens to a dripping faucet. What was the cause of Freeman's sudden, vertical decline? She stared absently at a dog crapping in constipated agony across the street, when she suddenly caught sight of her student friend. He had the same pallid and vacant look as Freeman, the same ghostly appearance. Without even thinking, the cause of it all was revealed to her. "He saw us holding hands in the tearoom," she cried and fled, leaving her friend gaping.

Meanwhile, miserable as ever, Freeman went home. He cast a listless glance at his bookshelves, his desk, his scant furniture, and halfheartedly made himself a cup of tea. He sipped it slowly, the way a hen drinks, munching on a tasteless biscuit in the same dispirited manner. This was how Mrs. Freeman found him. She begged to be forgiven for troubling him; her diffidence was genuine this time. Freeman floundered about, unable to decide where to put down his cup, how to get rid of his biscuit. He stared at her, dumbfounded. Mrs. Freeman regained her composure; she walked across the room and stood in front of the window, her back turned to Freeman. She remembered having seen films in which the heroine turned her back on the hero, or vice-versa, always, inevitably, gazing out of the window.

But having taken up this position, instead of finding herself gazing at pretty flower beds or a well-

tended lawn, as befitted a love scene, all she saw was
Freeman's old landlady laboriously hanging up faded
clothes on her washing line. Mrs. Freeman remained
silent for a few minutes, and then, in faltering tones,
she said she had a problem, and "please forgive me for
troubling you at such an inconvenient hour, I know
I haven't the right to impose on you, your time is
so precious," and more long-winded nonsense about
trust, experience, mature judgment, youthful foolish-
ness, and so on, after which she made as if to leave,
but not before throwing in en passant the phrase "and
that boy, you know, that fellow student of mine . . ."
To tell the truth, she made her way to the door so
slowly it took her about fifteen minutes to reach it.
When Freeman heard the words "fellow student," he
jumped up like a Jack-in-the-box; he certainly wasn't
going to let her leave the room; no, over his dead
body. "But of course," he said, "how could you possibly think, of course, you must tell me what's on your
mind, anything you like, God forbid, no, I'm not in
the least busy, friends in need are friends indeed,
God forbid." He kept on saying "God forbid" over and
over again, though the phrase didn't really connect.

He forced her to sit down on the sofa and rushed
into the kitchen to fetch her a whole tumblerful of
liqueur. "Speak, please feel free to speak, God forbid
. . ." Fine, I'm telling you all this while you lie in the

sun, but I've a feeling you're not paying much attention, you haven't made a remark for the last hour at least. All right, I agree, I did say you were not to interrupt, but there's no need to overdo it, a man needs some encouragement when he's telling a story, even if nobody asked him to tell it.

But I think we should take a dip in the sea, what with the ouzo and the heat I'm sweltering; even here in the cave I feel as if I'd just come out of the oven. Speaking of ovens I wish we had a nice leg of roast lamb with pasta and fresh tomatoes. To tell you the truth, I'm a bit fed up with baby squid. In the tavernas here they make them into something resembling fritters. Now what I do is simmer them in wine for three hours; that makes them beautifully tender. The food is impossible here in Batsi, always the same, day after day. Not that it's any better in Chora. All right, Chora is beautiful, I admit, but sad, like an old spinster in an old folks' home; as if it had been ravaged by a plague and abandoned, or as if it were under military rule, uptight and uneasy, with that awful giant statue of a sailor, somebody ought to throw it into the sea, it would make a perfect breeding ground for the fish. Shame on that sculptor, whoever he was, for producing that hideous thing; how he must have hated the working class, and especially sailors, to produce that monstrosity.

Well, now that we've cooled down a bit, let's get back to the story. Mrs. Freeman, glass in hand, started talking in a roundabout way about the student; the student this and the student that, he had fallen in love with her, but it wasn't her fault, perhaps she hadn't made things clear from the start, you know how it is at parties, an extra drink or two; in short, it was impossible to figure out what it was exactly that she was trying to make clear. Poor Freeman, she really put him on the rack, roasted him to a turn. Just as she seemed to imply that maybe she fancied the student, or at least wasn't yet sure how she felt about him, she did an absolutely masterly volte-face and declared she couldn't stand the boy, as a lover, she meant, she couldn't bear him touching her, and she needed Freeman's advice about what she should do to discourage him, in other words to send him packing. Suddenly the wretched Freeman glimpsed a whole resplendent horizon of happiness opening up before him. The heavens were rent asunder, revealing a triumphant sun. He felt like an Olympic champion, a decathlon champion to say the least—if I'm not mistaken that's the supreme event in the Games, for reasons I can't be bothered to explain right now—if not a gold medalist in swimming, sailing, karate and what-have-you. So he began pacing across the room, his head bent, pretending to be deep in thought to hide his exultation.

He advised her to be kind and patient, to give the boy sufficient time to get over his affliction. On the other hand, he said—proceeding to an indirect attack on the student and on younger males in general—she mustn't take the boy's feelings too seriously, by which he didn't mean that his feelings were not genuine, God forbid, no, the thought never crossed his mind, but one has to admit, from a purely objective point of view, that whereas young people are noted for their intense and often violent feelings, such infatuations, as Freeman chose to call them, are more often than not of short duration. As an afterthought, in his wish to exempt Mrs. Freeman from this sweeping generalization, he stressed that this applied mainly to young men; young women are more mature, he said, they seek a true companion in the person of their lover. So let her retain a friendly attitude towards the boy, but on no account encourage him further by agreeing to go out with him.

Mrs. Freeman gazed at him tenderly, wondering how a man so intelligent in all other respects could behave like an adolescent, and a virgin at that. She was overcome by a surge of pride: she had been right from the start in gauging the extent of her power. Now that her diagnosis was confirmed, she loosened up, a sense of quietude pervaded her being, a sweetness I might say, for Freeman's words were music to her ears, though she did not pay much attention to their meaning. Then all of a sudden she felt hungry.

No, I am not using Mrs. Freeman as a way of insinuating that I am hungry. It was only natural that she should feel hungry, like any normal person who hasn't enjoyed a proper meal for days—imagine a person who has been convalescing, faced with a couple of juicy chops sizzling on charcoal, to which you add a pinch of oregano at the last moment, taking care not to let them burn, meanwhile preparing a potato salad with a good dressing of oil, vinegar and a dash of mustard, together with some wild greens that grow on the mountains, you know, the curly kind with a slightly bitter taste, seasoned with plenty of lemon juice, and a chunk of warm bread to go with it. On the other hand, meatballs in fresh tomato sauce with spaghetti wouldn't be a bad idea, though they're a bit heavy on the stomach, make you sleep like a log, sink into oblivion, total annihilation, as if sucked down into the depths by tentacles.

Freeman went on to explain that bodily lust is undoubtedly one of the manifestations of love, but the actual duration of sexual desire still remains a matter of conjecture, and the same goes for the fixation on one specific sex-object rather than another; there are a number of factors that cause the body's physical desires to be ignored and convert what we call sexual love, Eros, into an imaginative process enacted in the mind. In his euphoric state, Freeman had turned uncontrollably garrulous. He warbled away, he sang, a constant stream of mindless nonsense pouring out of him in all directions. Instead of taking her in his arms and kissing her and telling her he loved her or something in that vein, instead of looking deep into her eyes and stroking her hair, he prowled around her as if she were an impregnable fortress, and hurled trivial verbal missiles at her. What was Mrs. Freeman to do? She simply accepted the evidence: her beloved was a bit slow on the uptake, besides what could you expect from a professor of linguistics, he was bound to choose the weapons he thought he was best qualified to use. Meanwhile Mrs. Freeman visualized a whole procession, a National Day parade of steaks, cheese pies, meat pies, spinach pies, walnut cakes, and even a humble crust of bread with olives; for I have observed that hunger is present everywhere, nature is hungry, grey mullet and baby crabs are desperately hungry, life itself is unbelievably hungry, life *is* hunger, for motion is the inevitable consequence of hunger, and let Freeman philosophize to his heart's content. In the end, Mrs. Freeman could contain herself no longer; she interrupted him a shade too abruptly and suggested they go and have a bite at the pub. She explained she had been so upset that she had been off food for days, so now she felt absolutely ravenous. Wait till I tell you what happened to *me*, said Freeman, and they burst out laughing in sheer relief. They dashed off to the pub hand in hand like bees hastening towards a patch of wild flowers.

Food and bed—what did you expect! They were in love, and they were hungry, greedy beyond belief! I never found out whether they made love that day. Mrs. Freeman told me she had never tasted such wonderful mashed potatoes or such succulent sausages as those they had at the pub. It was a memorable day, in spite of Freeman's shyness. He was always shy, she explained to me, I was always the one who had to take the initiative. They got married soon after that. Mrs. Freeman had no objection; in fact it amused her to think she'd go on being his student, her husband's student. Even after the wedding, she insisted on addressing him as 'sir' at the University, which naturally caused the other students to poke fun at her. They had no guests at the wedding; however, they duly observed the custom of going off on a honeymoon.

The morning after, they woke up in a large, expensive hotel room. The sun poured through the silvery curtains as if through a stage curtain. "I was truly happy," Mrs. Freeman told me. "No, it wasn't what you would call a strong intoxicating feeling, it was more like a giddy, light-headed mood, I laughed and laughed, I couldn't help laughing." Everything enchanted her, she even loved the tray with the remnants of their breakfast, she even ate up the crumbs of toast and croissants, she licked the honey off the little saucers with forget-me-nots on them, she nestled in his arms and wanted to coo like a dove, she listened to him telling her how he became a linguist and it was as if he were singing to her. It all began when he was fifteen, he said, on a trip to Egypt with his parents. They were a fairly well-to-do family, but always heavily in debt. His father always seemed to have far more financial obligations than assets. If he had lived, he might eventually have become rich, but a heart attack put a premature end to his career. Freeman went on to university, without any serious financial difficulties, for his mother became a living symbol of self-sacrifice; and as the ultimate token of her devotion, she conveniently died of cancer the moment her son settled down after graduating, at which stage she would only have been a burden to him. All she bequeathed to him were two wedding rings and her blessings.

It was during that visit to Egypt that he first set eyes on hieroglyphics. He mistook them for drawings, until he was told they were letters forming a complete alphabet. Illiterate dragomans assured him that nobody had been able to decipher them so far. Freeman began to dream he would be the first man to unveil the secrets of an ancient, defunct world. This dream still possessed him on his return from his Egyptian holiday, only to discover that a Frenchman by the name of Champlin, Champollion or something like that, way back in the eighteenth or nineteenth century—I don't exactly remember which, I'm no bookworm to go rummaging through the history of mankind, for all I care let the silkworms and mummies with their brains and insides scooped out go to hell—anyway, this Champollion character had already deciphered the Rosetta stone from the time of Ptolemy. You see, the same text existed both in Greek and in the hieroglyphic script, so Champollion had all the work made easy for him—big deal. Well, the dream of making a major discovery faded away, but in the meantime Freeman had fallen in love with words, all words, indiscriminately. He continued his studies with unabated passion; he believed that the entire world, known and unknown, consisted of a sequence of notions made up of words, and that in the last analysis the universe was simply a verbal construct rather than matter or energy or what have you. Mrs. Freeman, snuggling so close in his arms that she could hear his heart beating, suddenly realized that Freeman was not really a teacher, nothing of the sort, he was a tormented creature running after elusive words in order to discover some meaning to life. Brandishing an imaginary butterfly net, he was forever giving chase to an imaginary butterfly. He appeared to her defenseless, vulnerable; deeply touched, she kissed him on the nose. "Don't worry," she said, "I'll take care of everything." Freeman lowered his eyes shyly and smiled, as if asking forgiveness.

NICE PLACE, THIS. Ouzo may be bad for me, but I love it. Perhaps we should go and have our nap soon; look, all the others have left, I suppose they want their lunch, or perhaps the heat was too much for them. She's the only one left—that pale, flabby woman lying there, on the right, roasting away in the sun till she's as pink as cotton candy, she's sure to get terribly sunburnt. Well, let her. You know, as I sit here, on this patch of seaweed, like a prince on his magic carpet, I can feel it crawling with tiny insects, there must be thousands of them, I can feel them all over my body. My huge body must have disturbed them, every movement I make must seem to them like the shifting of continents, earthquakes registering over ten on the Richter scale, so they scurry around, demented, and sting me; I let my hand fall on all and sundry, but I've no way of knowing whether I've killed them or simply disabled them. You realize, of course, the terrific power I wield, far more than King Kong or those Japanese dragons that crush bridges with trainfuls of terrified little Japanese men and swallow supersonic jet planes and all that crap; this is something else, this is irrefutably real, no flight of fancy.

Mrs. Freeman must be about ninety years old now. Last time I saw her, she had the grave bearing of a person who has nothing to lose or to gain anymore. And even less to fear. It's true, she always spoke to me in a confessional tone. But in an impersonal way, mind you, not the way you talk to a friend or a person you respect and trust. I don't know what exactly it was she expected from me as I sat there listening to her; she didn't wish to entertain me, or merely convey information, that was perfectly obvious; she wasn't after my approbation either, she just talked to me without subterfuge or vanity, as if she were confiding in a diary, and what was more, without fearing an inquisitive eye might be reading over her shoulder. It was strange, you'd have thought she was talking to herself, as if I weren't there. She neither feared me nor despised me, she accepted me as something inevitable, as part of her life. At first, during our occasional meetings, she seemed to feel superior because she was so much older than me, but as time went by she gradually turned very timid and girlish; I believe she even blushed at times. But her shyness was all on the surface; as the years went by she grew bolder; in fact I am convinced that during the last few years, though she carried on with her confession, she had become totally oblivious of her confessor. I became aware of this because her eyes avoided me, looking right through me as if I were a windowpane, her voice sounding like an echo.

When we met, she didn't seem to have any notion of how much time had elapsed since our last meeting; she'd start her soliloquy at once, in a quiet yet almost bantering tone, touched with tenderness perhaps, as if she didn't really think her past was all that important. A mysterious compulsion to explain herself, I might say, but without any concern for what effect it might have.

I ENJOYED THAT QUICK SWIM. I love the sudden rush of water on the skin; its impact on the eyes, nose and ears; almost like all your orifices are being raped as you plunge in energetically. You soon get used to the water, though, and your breathing returns to normal as you swim along. Really nice. But let's have a bit of feta cheese. The bread may have been fresh from the oven when we bought it, but it goes dry in no time, so we'd better finish it before it goes completely stale. The heat, you see.

As I was telling you, then, soon after they married, they bought a house—the house in which her husband died, years later. Freeman, in a mood of boundless optimism, invested all his savings in this house. On the ground floor was the living room, the kitchen—facing east, spacious—and one more room which became Freeman's study. A lovely room, full of light, giving onto the peaceful little garden. The salon, as those of us who know French call it, had a large, very fine fireplace with multicolored tiles featuring tropical birds and intricate foliage; I never saw a fire burning in the grate; by the time I began visiting Mrs. Freeman she had already put in an electric heater. Not because she lacked taste, but she was getting old and felt the cold. On the second floor there were three bedrooms; one for the couple, with its own bathroom, and the others for their children, if and when they had any.

The couple's sex life could be described as pretty conservative. Though Freeman was a sensual man, he was more of a cerebral type really. Some kind of phobia or guilt got hold of him when he made love. He longed to have sex, but he couldn't help feeling relieved when it was over. I suppose he must have somehow connected sexual intercourse with urinating and defecating; the fact that the dark object of desire is situated in the same place as the apparatus for the disposal of urine and excrement generated revulsion in him. He enjoyed the soft porn that was in fashion at the time, postcards with semi-nude, plump, pinkish females, with one of their tits uncovered, waving goodbye to a crowd of invisible admirers with a handkerchief. He collected these postcards, most of them perfectly innocent, of course. Anyway, he did indeed desire Mrs. Freeman's body, he desired it passionately, but he also feared it.

When I met her, she was already old, so naturally I couldn't fathom what the hell Freeman had seen in this devastated flesh, how this moon-like face, these lackluster eyes could have inspired passion. I tried to visualize this wizened creature mincing, putting on girlish airs. I don't know why, but it was like seeing graves suddenly gape open to let out half-decayed corpses or skeletons dancing around, swathed in veils, pretending to be alive.

But we are not concerned here with whether or not Freeman was in love with the bodily ruin I have just described to you, nor are we really interested, come to think of it, in the love life of this man, who died suddenly of a stroke one quiet sunny morning.

He had just finished his breakfast, sitting in a pool of sunlight in the kitchen, reading his paper in a desultory fashion. Now and then he came upon an amusing item, and passed it on to Mrs. Freeman, who was carefully buttering her last piece of toast. All of a sudden Freeman sprang up and made a dash for the lavatory. As Mrs. Freeman took a sip of coffee, she heard a loud thud. "I told you not to climb on to the basin," she scolded, and ran to the lavatory. Opening the door, she found him folded over the basin with his trousers down.

All this happened years later, of course. For the time being, the newlyweds made love, but at the same time they were engaged in a deadly struggle; with the gentle determination of a surgeon who cuts you up for your own good, under total, partial, or no anesthesia, they strove to subjugate each other, to lacerate, to ingurgitate each other, beginning with the feet and moving upwards to gobble up the entire body—they were acting like cannibals, I tell you, their bed was that of Procrustes, in which each tried to cut down the loved one to size, to lead him/her by the nose. They were monsters of love, I'm telling you.

I'm beginning to feel really hungry, though. We've finished the cheese, there's just a little bread left, you have it. It's funny, but when I see you chewing, I get the distinct impression you're gnawing away at something, not just chewing. Anyway, Mrs. Freeman—like a contented cat with a mouse still writhing in her mouth, its tail hanging out—now got busy decorating the house, tastefully and with great gusto. And that wasn't all: she took up linguistics with unbridled enthusiasm, and then philosophy, and proved so good at both that Freeman no longer did anything without consulting her. To tell the truth, in one respect at least, Mrs. Freeman was superior to Freeman. She was fully aware of the terrible power that words exert on human beings. Freeman, being an expert, knew all about words, but he believed they were devoid of feeling. Fascinated by words, he forgot that they only acquired value through a human intermediary. Now this may be a facile pronouncement, because I never got to know Freeman after all, except through a few texts he wrote and his wife's account of him. However, I've come to the conclusion that he loved his work, but lacked imagination. He was only human, after all. He wasn't like me, blessed with a constitution that has made me a champion swimmer in the 100-meter free stroke, the 200-meter butterfly stroke, the 1500-meter breast stroke and the 400-meter medley, as well as a world record-holder in other events. He could never have done the marathon, as I did, in 30:04.00, or the pole vault, reaching 10 meters at the first try, and on the very same evening dance a pas de deux with Plissetskaya at Covent Garden. As our act came to an end, and just before fainting from sheer exhaustion, the great Plissetskaya exclaimed: "Oh my God, this cannot be, this has never happened to me before. Now I can die—at last I know what real dance is about." But then, I distinguished myself in every field, I even got the Nobel Prize, yes, indeed, the Peace Prize too, that just shows you. And the Oscar as well, all the Oscars in fact, for every role, good and bad, and all the special million-dollar awards handed out by multinational corporations and world organizations whose names I can't recall at the moment. No, Freeman lacked imagination, he belonged to the working class of language. His words waddled along like ducks, and they quacked like ducks, quack, quack, quack . . . The moment he became sure Mrs. Freeman loved him—and her marrying him gave him this assurance—he went back to chasing butterflies, that's to say, vain words. The couple lived in harmony, but their sex life presented certain serious problems. As Mrs. Freeman told me—reeling off her tale without pause, without so much as glancing at me—she had none of Freeman's inhibitions about sex; she wanted unlimited, unrestrained sex, she wanted to be raped, front and back, she wanted to scream, pant, writhe, to be drenched in sweat and sperm, to claw and be clawed at. No modest and discrete lovemaking in the dark for her, with few kisses and light caresses; no polite performance of marital duty, speechless and soundless, ending with a gentle kiss and off we go to sleep. Mrs. Freeman wanted to enjoy sex freely, naturally, the way you drink water when you're thirsty, dance in a disco, lick an ice-cream cone in midsummer in the noon heat. That's the way she wanted it.

But look here, I really think you should take a dip in the sea, you're like a shriveled octopus on the grill, go on, take a dip while I put some more seaweed under my ass, these stupid sea insects are giving me hell. And the seaweed—you'd think it keeps shrinking by the minute, soon I'll be sitting on bare pebbles.

As I was saying then, this is how Mrs. Freeman felt about it, but what was she to do? She tried, of course, she tried hard, but Freeman would get in such a state, he'd get so excited that he turned impotent. But her lust only grew more demanding, and God knows what it would have come to if she hadn't woken up one fine morning to find she was pregnant. True to her methodical nature, she immediately put aside her sexual yearnings and adapted herself to the new situation. Freeman's behavior at this time was terribly touching, she told me. Almost as if he were pregnant himself. He wasn't cut out for the role of lover; he was a born companion, a tender thoughtful mate, that was all. This was when she really became fond of him; but she never again looked upon him as a man.

She now went through a phase of inordinate greed. She ate incessantly, indiscriminately, as if preparing for hibernation. The days went by in a kind of sunny beatitude, without a care in the world. She felt like a great wild beast, a boa constrictor perhaps who has just swallowed its prey and proceeds to digest it in the secure knowledge of total possession. She watched over Freeman tenderly, fondled him, cared for him with unceasing vigilance, as if rehearsing her imminent motherhood. She had lost all traces of vanity; far from being bothered by her big belly, she examined it with unabated curiosity; she felt beautiful, regardless of what others might think. Her self-assurance and her lazy contentedness increased as the pregnancy advanced. She read a little, showed a desultory interest in what was going on, and took great pleasure in sleep. "You've no idea what you men are missing," she told me. "Pregnancy is a kind of sleep, but you experience it consciously, every minute of the time. Just for the sake of this sleep I wouldn't mind being pregnant for the rest of my life."

During those months, Freeman became a perfect candidate for dull fatherhood; he handled Mrs. Freeman like a rare Chinese vase from one of the earliest imperial dynasties. But at the same time he threw himself with renewed passion into his chosen field of study. He stayed up all night poring over

Egyptian texts, fascinated by hieroglyphic symbols, by squares represented by the letter Π, birds by the letter A and nooses by the letter O—which makes sense, after all—and generally applied himself to the pursuit of knowledge with unprecedented zeal. He'd rise from his desk at daybreak, having littered his study with the corpses of hundreds of disemboweled words, sighing like a man engaged in a losing battle, and he'd sneak into Mrs. Freeman's bedroom; there he'd bend over, listen to her breathing reverently, and with a weary smile deposit an ethereal kiss on her forehead, more like a prayer than a kiss; after which he'd withdraw, dissolving ghost-like into thin air.

"You know, Petros," Mrs. Freeman said, "when he sneaked into my room like that, I was almost always roused from my deep sleep; I was expecting a child, you see, and my body remained alert even in sleep; but I pretended to be fast asleep and let him leave the room without ever telling him how grateful I was for his quiet, undemanding love. Now that he is dead, I regret more than ever not having told him, because I can never make up for it. I'll always be sorry I didn't tell him."

I found Mrs. Freeman's outburst truly touching. I'm rather good at telling a genuine confession from a phony one; I happen to be in the unpleasant position of knowing what's what. This knack puts me at a disadvantage, because nowadays I find that fewer and fewer people are able to fool me; for the most part it's people who used to make me feel secure, life-enhancing people. I see through them now. How am I to go on living now that I've dropped them all, but mind you, without any ill feeling, without betraying their trust. It was my fault after all for having misjudged them, overestimated them; I am the one to blame, why should they be blamed for intentions they didn't even bother to disguise?

As I was saying, Mrs. Freeman was truly moved by her husband's tenderness. As for Freeman, after his silent pilgrimage to the conjugal bedroom, he would resume his linguistic battles with fresh vigor, as if newly baptized in a holy river, a pristine sea.

But look here, it's getting awfully hot in this cave, even though it's in the shade; so I think I'll go in and do the backstroke for five minutes. I enjoy doing the backstroke because what it really amounts to is floating on the water like a corpse, swaying gently to and fro. As a matter of fact, it would be nice to come out of the water and find a veal chop with French fries and two bottles of cold beer waiting for me.

Now that I am nice and cool, it occurs to me that sleep, I mean a good night's sleep, is bound to make your day go well. If you've had a bad night, you may think in the morning that you've got over it, but it lingers on, diffused through your whole body. But I've wandered away from my subject again, from Mrs. Freeman, who seems to have become a symbol for us all. I don't know why, but she's gradually assuming the aspect of an endless nightmare: the nightmare of a life made up of senseless details and repetitions. Well, let it be. To go on with the story: one fine day Mrs. Freeman gave birth to her baby. No big deal, you might say. A little boy. Ah, but what a boy. Unique in the whole wide world. All other babies had been born merely to bring out the uniqueness of her own infant. All other babies were no more than a floral décor, a stage set, something like a nativity scene, with her baby as the centerpiece: a small god.

She remembered nothing about the actual birth, not even the pain. She was told it was a boy, and that it was healthy and whole. Exhausted, she fell asleep. She plummeted into sleep like a dead body; she didn't even ask to see the baby. Next day they brought it to her, they told her it was hers, and she immediately started loving it. I must say there are things that I find impossible to understand. It's enough for a woman to assure a man that he is the father of a child, and a hospital certificate to assure a woman she's its mother, for a deep, unconditional, self-sacrificing love to be born. It's not a matter of instinct; they would be unable to tell their child apart from a bunch of other children. In brief, the idea of "my child" is completely optional. All you need is the will to believe. Come to think of it, here in my cool fragrant nest of seaweed, I'll be bold and say that it's not a question of whether the child is yours, but of not knowing that the child is not yours. But enough of this pseudo-philosophical twaddle. Mrs. Freeman eventually came home. She would dearly have loved to sleep with the baby, but a doctor friend said the baby should have a separate room. So they put the baby in the next room with the door wide open in case it cried. At this point she confessed to me that she began to hate Freeman, even though she knew it wasn't the poor man's fault. Well, it wasn't exactly hate, but a physical revulsion; she thought he smelled bad, she couldn't bear for him to kiss her or touch her, all she wanted was to sleep in the room next door with her baby in her arms. As the months went by and her indifference persisted, Freeman went into a kind of frenzy; he became importunate and wouldn't give her a moment's respite. In a certain respect, she felt flattered by his manic lust, his uncontrollable desire. He'd begin the moment they woke up; no sooner was she dressed than he would pounce on her, ready to tear off her clothes; he'd pull up her skirt and paw her frantically, clumsily; at lunch time, as soon as they finished their meal, he'd squeeze her into a corner. If she stooped to pick something up, he'd come up from behind and grab her, breathing heavily in that repulsive way of his, a feverish gleam in his eye. One day he even assaulted her in his study, just after she had brought him a cup of coffee; he flung his papers in the air, she told me, shouting at the top of his voice: "To hell with the Sumerians!" and threw her down on the floor and ejaculated on her thighs. Somehow her husband's bungling erotic euphoria made her intensely uneasy. This was the time when a younger colleague of Freeman's began to frequent their house; he courted Mrs. Freeman discretely, using various innuendoes and poetic quotations. She took to visualizing him as her lover; I mean to say, when Freeman made love to her she'd try to imagine this young colleague bending over her in Freeman's place. This helped her to put up with her husband's lovemaking. But in the end even imagination was no longer any help, so with an air of controlled hostility, of determined rejection, she forced him to give up and resort once again to his linguistic exertions. Of course, once or twice a month, she agreed to fulfill what is known as conjugal duties, simply for the sake of sticking to the marital pledge. Freeman went back to his role of aspiring suitor; he tentatively sought to win her back, to become her lover once again. But he strove in vain.

I suggest we take another dip; I feel so hot, it must be the ouzo. Well then, during this time Freeman turned into something of a ghost. He circulated in the house without looking right or left and only rarely addressed his wife; what their verbal exchanges boiled down to was a kind of coded language consisting of brief, workaday sentences. He kept to his study most of the time, and only emerged for meals, like a big mouse. He patted the baby with a smile—he was convinced it was to blame for the breakdown in his relationship with Mrs. Freeman—and then returned to his studies. He had become famous over the years, without fuss or fanfare. His fame went far beyond the limits of his professorial status at the University. He was now an international celebrity, a world authority on the languages of extinct civilizations. You would be hard put to find a scholarly book or paper that did not include phrases like "As Professor Freeman points out . . ." or "As Professor Freeman has so admirably demonstrated . . ."—in other words, he had acquired a prestigious reputation in the academic world. But he was a modest man, and an embittered one too: when he came home after his lectures or his brief travels, all he had to say to Mrs. Freeman was absentminded remarks like "yes, darling," "as you wish, darling," "you're absolutely right, darling," without any mention of his scholarly triumphs. He had become convinced that his wife no longer took any interest in him or his work.

Meanwhile the baby was growing fast into a little boy. Mrs. Freeman woke up one morning, like another Sleeping Beauty, and found the spell was broken. The bawling and yelling, the clamorous demands that used to captivate her gave place to a string of charming, babbling little words. It was no longer the same thing; the baby magic was gone. She was now confronted with a little person. The whole naked truth was suddenly revealed to her. Freeman had become famous, while she was no more than a well-behaved wife and an exemplary mother. She attacked him with unprecedented violence, accusing him of burying her alive, of reducing her to a mere housewife and deliberately concealing his success from her. For a whole year Freeman went through pure hell, with Mrs. Freeman's outbursts of rage culminating in shattered glasses and plates, slammed doors producing minor earthquakes. In the midst of these violent fits she flung further accusations at him: he had ceased to look upon her as a woman, he cared nothing about her love, her sexual needs; in other words, she placed the whole blame for her own aloofness on him. Things had now come to a head: Mrs. Freeman realized with horror that the family was falling apart, and that it was high time she put an end to her tantrums and change her behavior. No, you mustn't think she devised some diabolical plan; she simply adopted a number of ordinary safety measures. In the first place, she stopped nagging and complaining. A peaceful lull now reigned in the house. Windless calm on the high seas. Freeman basked in heavenly silence, which eventually turned into soft, tender susurration. Babbling brooks sang throughout the house, fluttering butterflies encircled it. Youthful impulses took wing, sudden fancies, such as taking a walk in the park, pausing by green ponds, visits to the museum; innocent laughter, wandering hand in hand, reminiscing over the past, well-known motifs like "do you remember the day it rained so hard we had to take shelter here, at this very spot?"

Which reminds me—do you remember that day in Venice, when we stepped out of our picturesque little hotel to go for a walk, our first walk in the city since our arrival—and the rain suddenly came pouring down, and we got shelter under the awning where a band was playing? I really enjoyed that, because I knew there was a nice hotel room waiting for us, and personally I was looking forward to a dinner of spaghetti and beer, followed by delicious sleep in anticipation of another heavenly day, when I would explore the city of the Doges and then start work on my new story, *Constantinople Has Fallen*.

Almost humbly, but with unflagging perseverance, Mrs. Freeman begged her husband to let her help him in his scholarly research, as they used to do in the early stages of their life together, when they still had a teacher-pupil relationship. During this lull in their marriage, a little girl was born to them. "I was serenely happy then," she told me. "No passions, no strong desires." This state of affairs went on for ten uneventful years, unmarked by any important happening apart from the normal changes you expect with children growing up in the house. This was the time when Mrs. Freeman bought frilly little curtains and generally gave her home its final, permanent look; these activities made her secure in the knowledge that she would die in her own bedroom, that she would always sit in her own sitting room, in a familiar refuge haunted by a multitude of voices—broadcasters, commentators, singers—and inundated by the flicker of endless serials and films; and that she would always wash in her own bathroom, sparkling clean like an operating-room, lavatory paper always at hand, complete with glittering mirror and fluffy towels; her own brightly lit, snow-white bathroom—in short, what she was actually doing was fitting out her ultimate burrow, her shelter, filled with paintings eventually made invisible by familiarity, though she would always know they were there, like big stains on the wall.

Nest building has always been a pleasant, soothing occupation. During this period then, the Freemans created a situation that gave them intense, though largely unjustified, satisfaction. Let me explain; they were both experiencing a kind of convalescence, as after a serious illness: the boundless pleasure in the mere fact of being alive, the blissful moment when pain, fever, medicines, and nightmares recede at last, and one fine morning, waking up in great shape, you come out with that marvelous, that divine phrase: "I am hungry." It goes without saying that this convalescent bliss is an entirely different thing from the active bliss of being in love. Yet nobody can say what makes one fall in love with a particular person, what chemical or other combinations, what unknown factors cause you to want Maria X rather than Maria Y. There's no way of knowing, and please don't go hunting for an explanation; I don't see why we should make a show of our ignorance.

So Mrs. Freeman became her husband's close collaborator. His colleagues accepted her as a scholar with a certain standing, but she never reached real eminence in the field, and sank into total obscurity soon after Freeman's death.

Meanwhile their little girl was quietly growing up; as for the boy, I'm not quite sure what he did. In fact, I don't seem to remember Mrs. Freeman mentioning her son while he was alive. If she did happen to utter the words "my son," she'd pause as if gulping down something, and her eyes would go soft and languorous, touched with sadness, I might say; a sadness that wasn't exactly painful, though, but more like nostalgia, like a memory of tenderness which saddens you because you know how it must end, yet there is a certain sweetness to it. When the boy grew up, there were fresh problems. Married couples, it seems, go through their good times and bad.

I can't make out if the ouzo they sell here is a medicinal spirit or the real thing. Well, never mind, we might as well have another. As I was saying, then, as soon as the children grew up, as soon as her daughter gave up dolls and concentrated on the size of her breasts, measuring them month by month, and as soon as her son began mentioning various girlfriends and coming out with statements like "she told me . . . so then I told her . . ." or "her parents won't let her stay out late, but if you think I'm going to hang around with babies . . . ," etc., putting on grown-up, macho airs, even though the poor boy hadn't even kissed a girl yet—as soon as all this came to pass, Mrs. Freeman realized the children-game was over, and she was the loser. The last blow, I think, the final confirmation came when she overheard her son saying on the phone, "I've got to hang up now, my old lady is going to give me hell." You must remember Mrs. Freeman was in her early forties then, and to use young people's vocabulary, she was still quite a hot number.

So she resigned herself to an embittered retreat. She began to lose interest in her home, her children; she watched Freeman with a certain resentment, because he didn't seem to take the slightest notice of his daughter's budding vanity or his son's erotic urges. If you want to know why—I mean, if you ask me whether he was a male chauvinist or something of the sort, not giving a damn about his family, well, I won't hesitate to reply, yes, he was. Freeman had settled down comfortably in his peaceful, well-run household; he felt there wasn't really much for him to do except air his opinions (which nobody listened to anyway), so he remained totally unaware of the crisis Mrs. Freeman was going through. She began to take a passionate interest in clothes, in underwear, too. Creams and lotions and other beauty products now cluttered the bathroom. Mrs. Freeman, who in her student days used to fling on any old sweater and sally forth into the street without as much as washing her face, now spent hours in front of the mirror, counting her wrinkles as if they were gold sovereigns, tugging her skin this way and that, massaging her arms and legs with various oils and ointments. Naturally, she couldn't help seeing that her skin wasn't what it used to be, but she believed it was because she hadn't taken enough care of it, not because of creeping old age. She also began to do daily exercises; she drank fruit juice, took vitamins, avoided fatty meat; she even stopped eating lamb altogether, gave up its crispy roasted flesh which she had once been so fond of. On the bathroom scale, she watched her weight like a hawk; in brief, she was on the look-out for a lover, and it goes without saying that when you put your mind to it you're bound to find what you are looking for. Mrs. Freeman was looking for a lover; and she found a lover.

This took place at an academic gathering, that is to say, a gathering of about forty or fifty linguists, which Mrs. Freeman had been unwilling to attend, because she was sick and tired of listening to various interpretations of words from the Etruscan, Persian or God-knows-what other language; in short, she was sick and tired of having to hear why people invented language and why they have always tried so hard to understand each other. But Freeman begged her to come along; a certain very important foreign scholar was to be the guest of honor that evening. Only for a short while, he promised, a mere act of presence, and then they would slip away without anybody noticing. Mrs. Freeman finally agreed. She chose the clothes she was going to wear with particular care, though without actually having a lover in mind; more like a fisherman casting his net just in case—if he catches some fish, so much the better. And then the miracle, so to speak, happened. A youngish man, not much younger than her, let's say six or seven years her junior, got into conversation with her; but instead of boring her with the idioms of the Mamelukes or some other dull talk, he began speaking about the lovely beaches of Greece, basking under brilliant sunshine (not for me, thank you); about nights at tavernas redolent with the smell of octopus grilled on charcoal; about ships sailing across still waters. But that was not why she fell in love; in short, it wasn't so much what he said that did it. This man had a nice face, a gentle smile; there was nothing aggressive in his manner, but Mrs. Freeman knew for sure that he was a lover. She sensed this at once, and she was not mistaken.

At this gathering, then, the guests drank cocktails, absentmindedly consumed canapés, and chattered away or laughed over well-worn jokes and anecdotes. About half-an-hour after their arrival, the thoughtful professor believed it was time he rescued Mrs. Freeman from her obnoxious interlocutor and the boring assembly as a whole. He went up to her and politely broke into the conversation with murmured excuses such as, "Unfortunately we have another engagement and I really think we ought to be going, darling, don't you?" But Mrs. Freeman wasn't at all prepared to give up her newfound flirtation. She replied that it was all right, they could stay a bit longer, they hadn't made a firm commitment with their friends, only a vague promise to phone them; she stared at him meaningfully, repeating emphatically that he'd got it all wrong, and stared back at him insistently, until Freeman grew confused and turned back in a daze to the group of people he had just said goodbye to. It was one of those eight to ten parties; the guests were beginning to leave, but Mrs. Freeman was lost to the world, absorbed in her flirtation as if watching a thriller on TV, while Freeman gaped vacantly at the waiters and the waiters stole glances at the other two talking in their corner. Finally Mrs. Freeman's admirer took matters in hand and suggested they all have dinner together somewhere. The three of them went off to a restaurant specializing in unusual seafood, as the man said. And so love was born, right under the Professor's sleepy eyes.

NOW I FEEL BEAUTIFULLY COOL. I can't bear the heat when I'm drinking ouzo. After a quick dip, what I like is sitting in the shade and letting the water slowly evaporate on my skin. So, as I was saying—the mere memory makes me laugh, but do cover your face, dear girl, you'll get badly sunburnt—Alex or George, or whatever her suitor's name was, called her the very next day; the sort of phone call customary in such cases: a cheerful voice, touched with tenderness, a carefree, playful voice with a faintly amorous undertone, of course, to which Mrs. Freeman responded with purring noises or a babyish twitter. A few days went by in this adolescent atmosphere of mutual erotic stimulation by telephone. Mrs. Freeman began to worry a little that the young man did not seem in much of a hurry to demand a private meeting. Later on, while they smoked the prescribed post-coital cigarettes, he explained that he had taken her for a rather prim and proper professor, who would need considerable time before agreeing to take off her clothes.

Their lovemaking was exactly what she had dreamed of as a newly-married girl. Their meetings began and ended practically without words. She would go to his house, and there they fought it out with loud groans and inarticulate cries. They bit each other, they licked each other frenziedly, writhed in violent sexual combat till their bodies ached; after which Mrs. Freeman would go home, a limp, fleeced creature. Come bedtime, she'd lie down like a vanquished gladiator and go to sleep like a baby, while

Freeman sat up reading some scholarly journal with almost clinical dedication.

"We didn't talk," Mrs. Freeman said to me, "our relationship was nonverbal. I would imagine him coming up to me with his clothes off, and I'd get all hot and flushed." They had turned into a pair of acrobats; they adopted the most strenuous positions, they grew increasingly brutal, beating and pinching each other till they were black and blue, biting into each other's flesh till they drew blood. Mrs. Freeman knew this sort of sex duel couldn't last. Her lover could never be a second husband. After three demented months, the passion was still there, but it assumed a kind of professional virtuosity, a perfect repetitiousness that no longer held any surprises. Perhaps it could have gone on a little longer if Freeman hadn't begun to display some rather odd symptoms.

What had happened? Well, Freeman the punctilious bureaucrat, the conformist who never cared much about his appearance, who always wore the right kind of suit with matching tie, emerged one morning in blue jeans, a light-colored sweater, white socks and sneakers. He installed an exercise bicycle in his room and religiously counted the imaginary kilometers he covered every morning; like his wife, he took to drinking fresh juices, gulped down vitamins and ate large quantities of fruit; and what was worse, he sang as he shaved in the morning the very songs he used to detest, songs like "Chiquita Mia, Do Not Torment Me" or "Suza, Suzanna, Amado Mio, Let Mañana Never Come."

Mind you, he was still the tenderest of husbands, in fact, more than tender, a perfect angel. He hastily agreed with her before she even had time to make a suggestion. He had sudden joyful outbursts, unaccountable fits of enthusiasm, but also bouts of depression, at which time he would shut himself up in his study saying he had work to do. But Mrs. Freeman was no fool; from the study window that led out to the garden, she was able to see that instead of working, Freeman just sat there holding his head in both hands as if fearing it might fly off, and stared stupidly at the wall. Mrs. Freeman realized then that her husband was in love, or at least something like that.

And, indeed, poor man, what was he to do, downgraded as a male and stifled by Mrs. Freeman's protective, motherly attitude; if you add to that the existence of her lover, who took up a considerable amount of her time, try as she may, and finally, the presence of two children, you'll see that he was practically relegated to fourth place or thereabouts, just something we're rather fond of, but in a comfortable, unworried way; we know it's ours, like a bank account, like a picture handed down to us by our parents, like our health, which we take for granted until we lose it, of course. In this set-up, then, Freeman was suddenly faced with the astounding discovery that his young female assistant was a twitter at finding herself working under the famous professor. "It flatters my vanity, that's all there is to it," he thought at first. Later on he came to the conclusion that it was rather pleasant to have one's vanity flattered. And this was how a minor love affair started between them, though it didn't last very long, as I gathered. He hadn't the necessary strength left to fall properly in love, he was emotionally burnt out. Mrs. Freeman and her iron rule over the household and the children had long since castrated him. Deep down, he didn't really desire anything except to be allowed to complain now and then.

Yet during his last brief bid to regain his lost youth, he found himself faced with new challenges. It wasn't so much that he didn't have the strength to fling himself into a great adventure; it was simply that he didn't believe in adventures.

And now that I come to think of it, it always strikes me as a sad thing to see so many of my acquaintances fatalistically accepting the fact that they have no future left, dragging themselves along from one day to the next without even grumbling, living side by side with their lifelong companion, a once great love now serving simply as something to cling to; like someone whose splendid yacht has sunk and who clings desperately to a life vest as the waves toss him around. But what does it matter, after all? Life is fun, and now that I come to think of it, man drowns in water and fish drown in air. What I mean is, I'm fed up with all this humanistic nonsense, what's it all about after all, why the hell must we love our own kind? I'm fed up, I tell you, but it's terribly hot, dear girl; I suggest we take another dip and then we'll pick up where we left off.

Have you noticed how cool you feel when you come out of the water, how pleasant it is, like thawing slowly after being in a deep freeze? I like that feeling. Now where were we, ah yes, then Mrs. Freeman panicked. She lost no time and issued a royal decree discharging her lover. She told him she loved him, but she couldn't wreck her whole life for the sake of a relationship that was bound to end soon, because of their difference in age, among other things. In the end her lover was not over-insistent, he was a bit upset, of course, probably because she had decided it before he did; he would have preferred to be the one to break it off, but on the other hand he felt relieved because their lovemaking—if you could call it by so gentle a name—was purely a matter of hygiene, a vigorous exercise of all their limbs, I'd say, gymnastics starting off with what amounted to mutual masturbation, but good for the circulation and consequently good for the heart. I read somewhere that people with heart trouble, or at least certain people with heart trouble, should have sex regularly. It is a prescribed thing, more or less like taking your pills regularly. It seems that a body deprived of sex soon withers away, and that is why masturbation, or jacking off, as illiterate people like to call it, far from being a harmful practice, does you a world of good; what's more it helps to flex the imagination. So Mrs. Freeman and Alex performed the exercise in question together, because anything one does is bound to improve when done in company; I don't know, but you get the feeling somebody wants you, loves you, shares your pleasure; not that this is what actually happens, most times, but what does it matter, as long as you believe it's so?

So the two of them parted; Mrs. Freeman realized the situation was critical: the girl not only possessed superior weaponry, her youth alone serving as a flying fortress, her breasts as atomic warheads, and add to this a radiant face, a bright, clear look, legs that could be swung up without the slightest effort to reach her chin—together with all this equipment, I say, Mrs. Freeman realized the girl also had another major advantage: she admired Freeman, whereas in his wife's eyes he was no more than a household object, something like a washing machine. But as I've already told you, and I've got to repeat it since you're so dense, Mrs. Freeman was certainly anything but dense. She immediately got organized. She began to drag him along to different cities on the pretext of attending conferences; she took him to museums, historical sites, famous old restaurants. She even went as far as neglecting her children. She had to bring down Freeman's temperature, to cure him. Not because of wounded pride or revenge; she loved him, she had never stopped loving him, but she had forgotten that fact. He was also a bit to blame for never reminding her. But it seems Mrs. Freeman miscalculated this time. Freeman followed her around with glazed eyes, his mind totally absorbed in this other budding Mrs. Freeman who had just emerged from her cocoon and now flitted about in his thoughts—a young, dazzlingly beautiful butterfly flashing the dire message: it's now or never.

"And so, Petros," Mrs. Freeman confessed with a sigh, "I had to accept this humiliating situation: knowing all about the affair, yet keeping silent." She rapidly switched tactics; no more endearments, fond looks, sweet nothings; no gentle bantering, but simply a discrete sharing of everyday life; the sort of attitude that prompts us to say things like: "Yes, as you wish;

very well, that's fine with me; don't let me disturb you; we'll talk it over tomorrow." She withdrew. But she kept an eye on things without seeming to. She waited patiently; she knew her man. No, he was no lover, he wasn't made of the stuff that arouses stormy passions, nor had he the vital force to experience passion himself, to forsake everything and forget all about words. Deep down she felt contempt for him; no, that isn't the right word, deep down she pitied him, she saw him—literally—as a worm, a bookworm slithering in and out of books, a puny hypochondriac falling into ecstasies over the present-perfect and the past-perfect tenses rather than over life; a weakling panicking at the sight of blood from a pinprick on his finger and rushing off to have a tetanus shot; to conclude, my personal view is that deep down, Mrs. Freeman never was in love with him. I don't have to say more, do I?—the affair with the girl gradually petered out, as you may have guessed.

There was no dramatic separation scene. Nothing like that. They just met less often, they both found excuses to put off spending an afternoon together; there was a kind of absentminded tenderness in the way they touched each other, until finally the girl went away on holiday. When she returned they tacitly stayed apart. Apparently they both accepted the parting with relief. The whole business, however, left the

Freemans with what I would call a mutual feeling of satisfaction. In other words, so to speak—I love using this phrase, "so to speak," there's something ironic about it, a sense of the futility of words and of any conclusions to be drawn from words, of course. If there's one thing that attracts me, it's managing to destroy seriousness; for instance, I love a sentence like "they had intercourse, and then he fucked her," where you see sheer ignorance of employing two words where only one is needed—I just love this confusion, this show of insolence towards words.

But I think it's time to have a dip. I've noticed for some time now that when I drop bread crumbs in the water, crabs dart out from under the pebbles; they grab the crumbs with their claws and try to drag them back to their holes, gobbling away as they go. And then grey mullet come along in droves from all sides and take their share of the crumbs. At such moments I feel the urge to say, "All things hast Thou created in Thy wisdom."

As I was saying, though, the whole business left both the Freemans with a sense of mutual satisfaction, so to speak. They had both had their fling, and this gave them self-confidence, the knowledge that they were still able to have love affairs, and what was more, with people younger than themselves. It made them feel they hadn't yet given up on life. The truth

was, however that they *had* given up, but they liked
to flatter themselves that they had done so of their
own accord. This was a time when they indulged with
total abandon in the minor pleasures of life. Mrs.
Freeman had never shown much interest in food; she
considered eating a rather boring business, necessary
but unimportant. Now, all of a sudden she began to
pore over recipes, to study sauces, to find out how to
marinate a rabbit; imagine, marinating a rabbit for
twelve hours, just to make a rabbit stew. She began
experimenting with meringues and caramel cream
and I can't quite remember what else, because I can't
bear sweet things. Anyway she went on to make com-
plicated salads, au gratin dishes, and God knows what
else; she stuffed zucchini with ham, with minced
meat, with rice, she stuffed chicken with spices, chest-
nuts and more rice, mixed with parsley, mint, onions,
and baked it for hours in the oven. She developed a
mania for cooking, and Freeman greedily ate everything she cooked, while inwardly reminiscing over
passionate scenes with his young assistant, without
any desire to repeat them, of course; he just ate away
unconcerned, I might even say he was almost happy.
Meanwhile he took only a statistical interest in his
studies, it seemed. Words no longer obsessed him;
he simply took care to keep up friendly relations with
them and nothing more.

He had given up trying to find out if words generate feelings or merely serve them. In fact, he wondered whether he really cared about the role of words and feelings, or the role of logic for that matter. I suffer in silence, he would say to himself, or I rejoice blindly, all the rest is a game to pass the time. So now Freeman sank voluptuously into gluttony, into a sensuous pleasure that required no companion; it involved only himself and his tongue, flavors that his mouth savored whenever he liked and as he liked. But once again, he had barely had time to settle down, to relax in his rounds of breakfast, lunch, dinner, when World War II broke out. His son joined the army, his daughter enrolled as a nurse. Food was rationed; it was enough to subsist on, but it was no longer something to be enjoyed. Those were the years I've told you about, remember, when as a child under the Nazi occupation, I got crippled with rheumatism and nearly starved to death, till I was literally reduced to skin and bones.

The Freemans lived on the outskirts of London. They planted sturdy vegetables in their garden, cabbages as hard as concrete; they even raised hens, carefully following the instructions in their farming manual. They heard news of the war, of course, but it didn't really affect them. The war finally caught up with them one morning, very discretely, in the form of the postman bringing them an official letter announcing the death of their son. It said he had fallen "in the service of his country," but eventually they found out he had been killed in a motorcar accident behind the lines. Mrs. Freeman confessed to me that she was disappointed hearing of his inglorious death; "a shameful thing," she said; she seemed to ascribe more importance to how he died than to the actual fact of his death.

She was very incensed at Freeman for keeping so calm on hearing that his son was killed. As for her, she refused to touch food for four days; she drank only water and wept without stopping. By contrast, her husband devoured his breakfast every morning, a shade absently, it is true, but that didn't stop him from gulping down his wife's breakfast as well. She began hating him, until she discovered that his coldness was nothing more than an attempt to set her a good example, to behave bravely, though Mrs. Freeman couldn't really understand the need for it. One morning, as she happened to be walking past the window of his study, she saw him holding his head in his hands and sobbing his heart out. She didn't breathe a word about it; at lunch time he ate with his usual appetite and drank his beer, chatting about the weather. "He had a different way of loving," she said, "which doesn't mean he loved less." As for their daughter, she had grown up without attracting much attention. During the war she fell in love with a young man who went off to fight somewhere, so she forgot him and fell in love with a middle-aged lawyer. She married him and disappeared to the United States. She never failed to send her parents Christmas cards. "I was fond of her," Mrs. Freeman told me, "but she was a very remote, reserved sort of person. I can hardly remember her as a child." And so the war years went by: their son dead, their daughter a stranger. "Ah well," she said to me, "that's the way it is, children are like beautiful toys, then one fine day they abandon you, and you're alone once more, right where you started."

The trouble was that the Freemans had also lost interest in their work. It had become a routine job like any other. In the general massacre of the war, who cared about the meaning—indeed, the deeper meaning—of words; who cared, at a time when words were defiled, cheapened: whores, dressed up as schoolgirls, I might say, pretending to be virgins, nuns devoted to God, when they were really nothing but brazen, aging whores.

As far as I could gather, during those years they got used to the idea of living without looking forward to anything in particular. They were neither happy nor unhappy. They were devoid of ambition, and, naturally, of expectation. Each day had to be lived for itself, it was all there was. They read the papers, picking out only items about crime or the arts; they also scanned the social column because it featured well-known people. They never bothered to vote, having reached the conclusion that elections ought to be abolished and the country run by senior civil servants with a long record of efficient service. Promotions would be based on selection among candidates with equally high qualifications. In this way, they said, the prime minister would serve for a number of years as a sort of general coordinator, but in effect the state would be self-governed.

As time went by, however, Mrs. Freeman began to worry about her age. She turned her attention to her wrinkled neck, her arms and legs; she studied her cellulite with intense concentration. She showed a sudden concern for a healthy diet; she bought various cereals, black bread, skimmed milk, beverages containing Vitamins A, B, and C, all that sort of stuff, you know the kind I mean. She counted calories carefully, forced herself to drink one quart of water a day, perused her morning stool and literally made Freeman's life hell. He ate without protest all that insipid muck, which may well keep the body fit, I agree, but which destroys the appetite for life.

No, but listen, if I have to run in and out of hospitals all my life for tests, checking one thing after another just in case my X has gone up or my Y has gone down, I'd rather not know and meet my end in blissful ignorance. All right, I don't mind sticking to a certain treatment if the need arises, but I can't spend my life worrying about my cholesterol, my blood pressure, my urine, my kidneys, my adrenal glands, my pancreas, my liver, my muscles, my nervous system, sympathetic and parasympathetic—I just won't, I tell you, so there.

Well, the Freemans went on consuming broccoli and cauliflower, celery and okra (which are chockfull of Vitamin A), green peppers, radishes, zucchini, beetroot, dandelion, spinach, turnip greens—can you imagine?—greens of all kinds, whole-wheat bread, fruit containing only a minimum of carbohydrates, and God only knows what else. Mrs. Freeman could tell you exactly how many calories there are in two medium-sized apricots, half a banana, ten large cherries, two medium-sized dates, God help us, one large fig, and—you may well gape—twelve medium-sized grapes. Mrs. Freeman was waging war against old age. During this stage of their lives Freeman stopped writing; but he still corresponded with other distinguished linguists. After World War II, it was discovered that a good number of words had lost all meaning, not to mention the fact that several were now considered outlawed. So he spent most of his time in his study, and showed no interest at all in Mrs. Freeman's vapid health food. I've no way of knowing whether he still loved her or simply put up with her as one does a nurse or a mother. Anyway, from what I gathered he remained a compliant husband.

It was at this point that Mrs. Freeman began loving him again. She loved him passionately, as if he embodied her future, her children, the children she no longer had: the dead son, the ungrateful daughter whom she only remembered when she was feeling disgruntled. Freeman now represented her whole life. She watched over him anxiously, she looked after him, she loved him so much that she even monitored his breathing. Freeman had become her sole purpose in life. The once ambitious Mrs. Freeman helped him with his work; she rummaged through books, dictionaries, scholarly texts, reports on ancient cultures, all for the sake of giving Freeman time to correspond with his fellow scholars but also in order to induce him to rise from the position of adviser and commentator to that of a true scholar with theories of his own.

They had shaped a new life for themselves, I might say, not necessarily a happy one—let me be, for God's sake, don't give me this stupid word *happiness,* a word we've discovered as the surest way to make ourselves unhappy—as I was saying, then, they had found a sort of happiness, when Freeman was taken ill suddenly—a sharp pain in his chest and two bouts of vomiting. As I've already told you, Mrs. Freeman was a sensible woman, no foolish, banal little housewife, she. She immediately diagnosed a heart attack, and she was right; in fact, it was a severe heart attack. In Mrs. Freeman's eyes her husband's status changed from child to infant. She fed him his meals, she placed his pills in his mouth, she watched over him like a huge vulture protecting its brood. Freeman lost the last shred of the privacy he had enjoyed in his study. Mrs. Freeman's love turned into what most naive people probably dream of: absolute love. Power. Unwittingly she also began to identify herself with Freeman. She followed the same diet; she stopped smoking; she felt tired whenever Freeman felt tired. They lost weight together, and eventually their movements, their voices, their reactions, their expressions, their laughter became so alike that even their faces began to resemble each other. Perhaps they were approaching a state of total fusion, a realistic confirmation of "they shall be one flesh," when disaster struck again. It was a hazy spring morning; the glass-enclosed room was bathed in light; mild, pale yellow sunlight, gentle as a caress.

I don't know why this image comes to my mind; sunlight filtering through a glass-paneled veranda, through which one glimpses a small garden caught in a windless calm, as in a photograph. The patches of green are very bright, a few tiny flowers are shyly budding forth, some kind of insect sticks to the crystal-clear glass, revealing its belly, then suddenly flies off in an unknown direction. This image makes me feel I'm a small child in some strange house which I'm sure I've never visited; yet I have the feeling that I once was in such a house with a glass-paneled veranda. It was a fine spring morning, and I stretched out my hand to steal a round sugary biscuit from a bowl on the bamboo table. It's a purely imaginary scene. My hand is suspended in midair over the bowl of biscuits, but it's as if I were stealing with the permission, or at least the tacit consent, of some grown-up, my mother perhaps; I cannot see her, but I can sense her presence.

Mrs. Freeman was telling me then that it had been a divine morning, she felt a peaceful happiness pervading her whole body as she finished eating a slice of bread with margarine and honey. She described the cactus on the ledge with its fleshy green leaves, the white tablecloth, the crockery speckled with little roses. She was smiling, she was bathed in bliss as she admired the details of the scene. Freeman idly scanned the morning paper and made occasional comments, after emitting a phony little laugh to attract her attention. She gazed at him and repeated happily to herself, "I love you, you silly thing, poor silly old thing, a lifetime together, my old darling; now we've grown old, my darling silly old thing." She recounted all this to me with an angelic smile, lost to the world, as if I were Freeman; then suddenly a cold shadow descended over her face. "Freeman got up," she said, "apologizing: 'I'll be back, nothing to worry about,'" he said. He ran to the bathroom; Mrs. Freeman heard a loud thump; in the midst of enjoying the sunshine, she experienced something like an earthquake. She found him folded over, the upper half of him hanging over the lavatory, the lower half leaning against the wall, his trousers and underpants down.

"We buried him," she said, "and then we were left all alone"; she used the plural "we" as if the dead man had been a third person. "Now he is gone, there is no longer much for us to do. I still resent him for leaving us. I know it's unreasonable, but I still resent him. He shouldn't have done that to us. His silence after he died seems like contempt."

At first she kept seeking him out in the bedrooms, the garden—in his study she very nearly thought she saw him. She placed pictures of him all over the house; she talked to him. Nothing dramatic, mind you. She talked about everyday things, the weather, the shopping, their friends. After a few years, the photographs disappeared. "They didn't represent Freeman anymore," she said to me. He had become a stranger, a hostile stranger, in fact. He stared at her stupidly, she said, as if he didn't realize he had died.

She gradually picked up her old habits again. She resumed her anti-heart attack diet. She continued to correspond with his colleagues. The last time I saw her she was past ninety. She sat with her hands crossed and smiled at me with what I might call an ominous serenity. "Funny boy you used to be," she said. "I was always fond of you. You had a natural curiosity about things, but you were never rude; natural good manners."

I was struck by the fact that she addressed me as if I were no longer alive. Perhaps she had filed me away in her past along with the rest.

With an ingenuous smile I asked her:

"By the way, I've been wanting to ask you, what is it you really want in life? What does Mrs. Freeman want now?"

"Everything."

B UT NOW I SUGGEST we take one more dip, and then we can go and have our afternoon nap.

about the author

Petros Abatzoglou (1931-2004) grew up during the Nazi occupation of Greece and traveled extensively in Europe and America during his 30s before settling in Greece until his death. In addition to his writings for newspapers and the radio, he is the author of numerous short stories and several novels, including *Death of a Salaried Man*, *Pavlos and Eleni*, *The Birth of Superman*, and *Balance of Terror*, for which he received the Greek National Book Award in 1965. He also received the National Book Award in 1988 for *What Does Mrs. Freeman Want?*, which is his first book to be translated into English.

SELECTED DALKEY ARCHIVE PAPERBACKS

FOR A FULL LIST OF PUBLICATIONS, VISIT:
www.dalkeyarchive.com

SELECTED DALKEY ARCHIVE PAPERBACKS

CAROLE MASO, *AVA*.

LADISLAV MATEJKA AND KRYSTYNA POMORSKA, EDS.,
*Readings in Russian Poetics: Formalist and
Structuralist Views*.

HARRY MATHEWS,
The Case of the Persevering Maltese: Collected Essays.
Cigarettes.
The Conversions.
The Human Country: New and Collected Stories.
The Journalist.
My Life in CIA.
Singular Pleasures.
The Sinking of the Odradek Stadium.
Tlooth.
20 Lines a Day.

ROBERT L. MCLAUGHLIN, ED.,
*Innovations: An Anthology of Modern &
Contemporary Fiction*.

STEVEN MILLHAUSER, *The Barnum Museum*.
In the Penny Arcade.

RALPH J. MILLS, JR., *Essays on Poetry*.

OLIVE MOORE, *Spleen*.

NICHOLAS MOSLEY, *Accident*.
Assassins.
Catastrophe Practice.
Children of Darkness and Light.
The Hesperides Tree.
Hopeful Monsters.
Imago Bird.
Impossible Object.
Inventing God.
Judith.
Natalie Natalia.
Serpent.
The Uses of Slime Mould: Essays of Four Decades.

WARREN F. MOTTE, JR.,
Fables of the Novel: French Fiction since 1990.
Oulipo: A Primer of Potential Literature.

YVES NAVARRE, *Our Share of Time*.

DOROTHY NELSON, *Tar and Feathers*.

WILFRIDO D. NOLLEDO, *But for the Lovers*.

FLANN O'BRIEN, *At Swim-Two-Birds*.
At War.
The Best of Myles.
The Dalkey Archive.
Further Cuttings.
The Hard Life.
The Poor Mouth.
The Third Policeman.

CLAUDE OLLIER, *The Mise-en-Scène*.

PATRIK OUŘEDNÍK, *Europeana*.

FERNANDO DEL PASO, *Palinuro of Mexico*.

ROBERT PINGET, *The Inquisitory*.
Mahu or The Material.

RAYMOND QUENEAU, *The Last Days*.
Odile.
Pierrot Mon Ami.
Saint Glinglin.

ANN QUIN, *Berg*.
Passages.
Three.
Tripticks.

ISHMAEL REED, *The Free-Lance Pallbearers*.
The Last Days of Louisiana Red.
Reckless Eyeballing.
The Terrible Threes.
The Terrible Twos.
Yellow Back Radio Broke-Down.

JULIÁN RÍOS, *Larva: A Midsummer Night's Babel*.
Poundemonium.

AUGUSTO ROA BASTOS, *I the Supreme*.

JACQUES ROUBAUD, *The Great Fire of London*.
Hortense in Exile.
Hortense Is Abducted.
The Plurality of Worlds of Lewis.
The Princess Hoppy.
Some Thing Black.

LEON S. ROUDIEZ, *French Fiction Revisited*.

VEDRANA RUDAN, *Night*.

LYDIE SALVAYRE, *The Lecture*.

LUIS RAFAEL SÁNCHEZ, *Macho Camacho's Beat*.

SEVERO SARDUY, *Cobra & Maitreya*.

NATHALIE SARRAUTE, *Do You Hear Them?*
Martereau.

ARNO SCHMIDT, *Collected Stories*.
Nobodaddy's Children.

CHRISTINE SCHUTT, *Nightwork*.

GAIL SCOTT, *My Paris*.

JUNE AKERS SEESE,
Is This What Other Women Feel Too?
What Waiting Really Means.

AURELIE SHEEHAN, *Jack Kerouac Is Pregnant*.

VIKTOR SHKLOVSKY, *Knight's Move*.
A Sentimental Journey: Memoirs 1917-1922.
Theory of Prose.
Third Factory.
Zoo, or Letters Not about Love.

JOSEF ŠKVORECKÝ,
The Engineer of Human Souls.

CLAUDE SIMON, *The Invitation*.

GILBERT SORRENTINO, *Aberration of Starlight*.
Blue Pastoral.
Crystal Vision.
Imaginative Qualities of Actual Things.
Mulligan Stew.
Pack of Lies.
The Sky Changes.
Something Said.
Splendide-Hôtel.
Steelwork.
Under the Shadow.

W. M. SPACKMAN, *The Complete Fiction*.

GERTRUDE STEIN, *Lucy Church Amiably*.
The Making of Americans.
A Novel of Thank You.

PIOTR SZEWC, *Annihilation*.

STEFAN THEMERSON, *Tom Harris*.

JEAN-PHILIPPE TOUSSAINT, *Television*.

ESTHER TUSQUETS, *Stranded*.

DUBRAVKA UGRESIC, *Lend Me Your Character*.
Thank You for Not Reading.

LUISA VALENZUELA, *He Who Searches*.

BORIS VIAN, *Heartsnatcher*.

PAUL WEST, *Words for a Deaf Daughter & Gala*.

CURTIS WHITE, *America's Magic Mountain*.
The Idea of Home.
Memories of My Father Watching TV.
*Monstrous Possibility: An Invitation to Literary
Politics*.
Requiem.

DIANE WILLIAMS, *Excitability: Selected Stories*.
Romancer Erector.

DOUGLAS WOOLF, *Wall to Wall*.
Ya! & John-Juan.

PHILIP WYLIE, *Generation of Vipers*.

MARGUERITE YOUNG, *Angel in the Forest*.
Miss MacIntosh, My Darling.

REYOUNG, *Unbabbling*.

LOUIS ZUKOFSKY, *Collected Fiction*.

SCOTT ZWIREN, *God Head*.

FOR A FULL LIST OF PUBLICATIONS, VISIT:
www.dalkeyarchive.com